ONE NIGHT ONLY

JC HARROWAY

MILLS & BOON

First Published in Great Britain 2018
by Mills & Boon, an imprint of HarperCollins*Publishers*
1 London Bridge Street, London, SE1 9GF

© 2018 JC Harroway

ISBN: 978-0-263-93220-1

MIX
Paper from
responsible sources
FSC www.fsc.org **FSC° C007454**

This book is produced from independently certified FSC™ paper
to ensure responsible forest management.
For more information visit www.harpercollins.co.uk/green.

Printed and bound in Spain
by CPI, Barcelona

To E
for inspiring the fun, bubbly, caring Essie. x

CHAPTER ONE

IF THIS SETTING, so far from the wreckage he'd left behind in New York, couldn't provide ballast, nowhere could. Ash Jacob closed his eyes, sucked in a deep breath and focussed on the sun warming his back, the hypnotic chatter of English birdsong and the continuous distant hum of London traffic.

'Shit!'

The violent exclamation pulled him up short. So he wasn't the only one having a bad day. His vision hazed as the bright July sunlight hit his retinas once more, his surroundings sharpening into focus. He stretched one arm along the back of the park bench, the wooden slats of which dug into his fatigued muscles—a reminder that he'd spent twelve hours on a plane yesterday, largely bent like a pretzel despite his first-class seat.

'Bloody, buggering, shit.'

What a charming turn of phrase.

His mouth twitched and his mood lightened. She stood a short distance away from his secluded spot in St James's Park, her short, flowery dress revealing bare, shapely legs; golden hair streaked with enough russet to turn her long ponytail to fire in the right light; a small denim backpack slung over one shoul-

der, which made her appear younger than what he es-
timated as mid-twenties.

A student? A tourist? A fellow soul, far from home?

One delicate finger jabbed at the screen of her
phone, as if she could poke it back to life by dogged
persistence alone.

Intrigue and a flicker of lust made Ash sit up
straighter. Her quirky English accent and endearing
choice of expletives reminded him that New York was
a long way away. And yes, the women in his exclusive, affluent circle had the kind of polish and poise
that this beguiling stranger seemed, at first glance,
to lack, but the effect of the jut of her pert breasts
and the cut of her fine-boned features in profile on
his jet-lagged libido equalled, if not surpassed, his
usual level of interest in the opposite sex. An interest
that circumstances had shaped into two simple rules:
one—on his terms; and two—one night only.

He shifted on the hard seat, his jeans becoming skintight, at least around the groin. The beauty
dropped the hand holding the offending device to her
side and cast her wide eyes around their corner of
the park.

Ash slammed his own stare closed again, pretend-
ing to enjoy the formerly relaxing ambience. He'd
come to London to work on a joint business venture
with his oldest friend, not to rescue an English dam-
sel, no matter how long her legs or how curvaceous
her ass. And more importantly, he'd come to get away
from public drama and get his life back under control.
Control that couldn't come soon enough.

'Um, excuse me...'

Damn.

She'd moved that delectable derrière of hers closer. There were few people around, mainly joggers and the odd parent pushing a stroller. She *must* be talking to him. Ash relaxed his eyelids and slowed his breathing. Perhaps if she thought he was asleep, she'd leave him alone. Find someone else to rectify her technology issues.

Her footfalls scuffed the gravel of the path.

There was an embarrassed tinkle of laughter.

Right in front of him now.

Close enough for her scent to tickle his nose— light, floral and mixed with the unmistakable smell of sunscreen.

His libido roared anew. Man, would he love to see those curves and that milky skin clad in a bikini and sprawled on a lounger at his holiday place in the Hamptons.

The sexy intruder delicately cleared her throat.

The sweet sound rolled over his out-of-sync senses. Physically, she embodied the epitome of his type. Under other circumstances, he'd turn on the charm, get to know her enough to assess if her persuasion for no-strings sex aligned with his, and pass a satisfactory afternoon between her thighs.

But the last thing he needed right now was an encounter with a woman *that* beautiful, especially one who awoke his interest to the degree currently rendering him momentarily trapped on the park bench by his tight jeans.

He'd been played in the past—the old, female-inflicted wound recently reopened in the most humiliating and public way being the main reason for his rather hasty departure from New York.

For now, women were categorically off the agenda.

And really, who talked to complete strangers in a city centre park? His appearance today could only be described as dressed down compared to his usual attire of bespoke tailored suits. He'd wanted an escape from the cloying, air-conditioned hotel he'd booked for his first couple of nights in London until the Jacob Holdings apartment had been spring-cleaned. Some fresh air. Green spaces. Anything that helped to reprogram his brain from its current gut-churning cycle of guilt and bile-inducing self-loathing.

So he'd thrown on a T-shirt and his comfortable jeans, both the worse for wear having spent forty-eight hours in a suitcase, forgone shaving off the three days' worth of scruff and headed outdoors. The casual look was a visual cue that his move to London represented a major change from the norm; a shift from everything he'd lived, breathed and strived for these past ten years: his role in the family business, which was fraught with dysfunctional politics in the hands of his ruthless, manipulative and, as he'd bitterly discovered in the most degrading way, cheating father.

'Excuse me, are you…okay?'

Ash surrendered to the soothing voice with a sigh that dragged his mind back from the edge of a dark abyss. She wasn't going to give up. Perhaps she was lost. He didn't know London that well, but he'd spent enough time here over the years to have a vague sense of direction. Better to hear what she wanted and send her gorgeous ass on its way.

He opened his eyes, forcing his face to exhibit a tight, inquisitive smile instead of the frustration that put his teeth on edge at having the embodiment of feminine temptation literally thrown into his path.

'Of course. Just enjoying the sun.'

Her answering beam had two opposing effects on his overwrought body: the fullness of her pouty lips direct-messaged his groin with a slug of not wholly un-welcome blood-pounding heat, and her open, friendly stare twitched his shoulders up several notches until his muscles cramped. Were all English women this naive? This trusting? For a man who trusted no one, she was a complete mystery.

'Oh, good. I don't suppose I could ask for a fa-vour...?' She waggled her dead phone in front of his face. 'My phone just died.'

'Okay... Are you lost?'

Give her some damn directions and watch her groan-worthy legs walk away.

But then his view would be far less appealing.

Another megawatt smile warmed his insides and made him think of childhood trips to Coney Island.

'No. I wondered if you could take a picture for me.' She pointed at the view of the London Eye in the distance. 'On your phone...and perhaps...send it to me?' Her voice wavered and she curled some escaped strands of hair at her nape around her index finger.

His expression must have been comical. Had he woken up in some parallel universe or was her friend-liness some sort of ancient British ritual? Did he care if it meant a few more seconds surreptitiously eyeing her glorious body and fantasising about her naked under him?

Ash shifted, discreetly readjusting himself in his pants as he allowed his gaze to properly take in every inch of porcelain beauty. Up close, she was stunning. Flawless creamy skin, enormous sky-blue eyes and a charming dusting of copper freckles across her slightly upturned nose. And on first impressions— the embodiment of a sunny disposition.

And if she wanted a photo, she was clearly a tourist. Perhaps this was her last day in London?

Another point to his libido.

As if matching his interest, she flicked her stare over him from head to toe, skimming over his creased tee and well-worn jeans and flooding his body with heat to rival the summer sun. Was she flirting?

'Sure,' he said.

Why not? He could surely oblige her with a photo and perhaps anything else she might want. He lifted one eyebrow as her eyes returned to his face. Bright spots of red appeared on her high cheekbones as she straightened the charming little head tilt she'd employed while checking him out. Yes, perhaps she was exactly what he needed… A little help with his current hard-on predicament. She seemed to share his physical interest. Perhaps that would cure his mind-numbing restlessness and get his usual focus back on track.

The tension snapped with her tinkling laughter. Ash grinned back. At least she owned her flagrant sexual curiosity in him—how refreshing. He reassessed her age—perhaps she wasn't as sweet as she looked. She flicked her ponytail, sunny smile back in place.

He shifted on the bench, fishing his phone from his back pocket. The angle of the sun meant her dress was practically see-through from his position. Should he tell her? Or just enjoy her shapely silhouette? Imagine those long legs wrapped around his waist…

No.

His mind zapped to ancient history come back to haunt him. His recent discovery of the lengths his ex had gone to in order to deceive him, and the depth of that lie, only confirmed his stand on the opposite sex. He was done with women, unless they, like him, wanted one thing only and understood the rules.

The weathered wooden rungs of the bench creaked as she sat next to him. 'You're American, aren't you?'

He nodded and then looked away from her open, earnest face. At least this woman couldn't be interested in the prestige and power of his family name or his considerable personal fortune, dressed the way he was. She couldn't know his family owned half of Manhattan and a sizeable chunk of London. She couldn't guess he'd come to London to distance himself from his 'real estate tycoon' reputation—as well as from the ruthless deception by one family member in particular. Not unless she read the society pages of the *New York Times*.

He tasted bile. How could his father do that to him? To his own son? Making a mockery of the years of professional loyalty Ash had given the family business? Fuck—did he have 'trusting schmuck' stamped across his forehead?

The sexy stranger didn't seem aware of his inner turmoil. She turned her body to face him so her bare knees bumped his denim-clad thigh, eyes alight. 'London is an amazing city, isn't it? Have you seen Buckingham Palace? It's just over there.' She pointed over her shoulder, warming to her change of subject and speaking with dizzying speed in her excitement about the tourist attractions the city had to offer.

'And do you know about the Seven Noses of Soho? I'm scouting them out today. Fun fact…' She pointed towards the small lake in the park. 'Did you know the pelicans were a gift from a Russian ambassador to King Charles the second in 1664?'

She talked so quickly, her charming accent distorting the English until she might as well have been speaking Mandarin. Noses? Pelicans? Perhaps the impotence coiled inside him was steadily infecting and destroying his brain cells. Perhaps he was more jet-lagged than he'd assumed. Perhaps testosterone had fried his usual laser-sharp mind.

'So, you wanted a picture?' He unlocked his phone and leaned forward, preparing to stand. Do a good deed for the beautiful English rose so he could get on with trying to cobble his shit back together. He could no longer pretend that his sole motivation for coming to London was for a new business opportunity. Other factors had made him flee across the Atlantic—his guilt at forcing his mother to face her sham of a marriage, and the shameful publicity that had followed his bust-up with his father. Belonging to a high-profile family had its distinct downsides.

But he'd left all that behind.

Focus on the here and now.

London, the rich culture and vibrancy of the city, provided abundant distractions, though none quite as appealing as the distraction warming the sliver of space between her body and his and momentarily taking his mind from his troubles.

'How long have you been here?' Another head tilt, her tongue peeking out to swipe her lower lip.

A silent groan rattled his skull.

So not fair.

'A day or two.' How could he ignore such delicious temptation right in front of him? Surely he'd read her signals correctly. The perfect diversion sat before him looking at him as if he were a tasty snack—what could be more temporary than two travellers making a connection and enjoying one lost night in London?

No need to confess his real identity—one of New York's top corporate attorneys, a real estate mogul and heir to the Jacob fortune. Not that he wanted to publicise any association with his bastard father right now. Hal Jacob's ruthless streak had long made Ash wince. But even he hadn't seen the train wreck approaching, hadn't anticipated the far-reaching, closer-to-home consequences.

He scrubbed his hand over his face, forcing his dark thoughts to take a sharp left turn, and focussed on the enticing, quirky and sexy woman in front of him. She smelled fantastic. Just the thing to settle the out-of-control spiralling of his thoughts,

Yes, she was a little greener than most of the women who passed briefly through his life, but just as striking. Practically the polar opposite of the sophisticated women he usually invited into his bed, her bubbly personality was as intoxicating as a breath of fresh and fragrant summer air. The flicker of interest in his groin built, stirring his limbs with urgent energy.

Ash covertly checked her ring finger—bare.

But in his experience, women who looked like her—

peaches and cream complexion, whimsical ponytail—wanted more than he was willing to offer. Wanted a relationship. And he never went there, no matter how appealing the inducement.

Not since his ex-fiancée…

Ash stood in an attempt to banish the jitters in his legs. He'd take her damn snap and put an end to this weird Transatlantic lesson in charming, but eccentric, cultural differences. Remove himself far from temptation.

He stepped into the centre of the path and raised his phone to the distant iconic view of one of London's most popular tourist attractions. With a click he'd completed his obligation, his intentions still wavering between polite dismissal and revealing some of his cards in case he'd been wrong about her and she shared his philosophies on casual sex.

'Have you taken the ride?' She appeared at his side, her eyes focussed on the giant wheel, its half-glass pods glinting in the sun.

'Not yet.' He held out his phone for her inspection, his mind flitting to a different kind of ride as she leaned close to stare at the screen and the tips of her silky hair glided over his wrist.

Fuck! No amount of English fresh air was going to shift this…urge. And, away from the negotiation table, Ash was never more in control than in the bedroom.

Yes, a little summer loving would both banish his restlessness and put his head straight. Hopefully, the control he demanded in the bedroom would re-infect the rest of him and shunt him back onto an even keel in time for the first day of his new business venture tomorrow.

The captivating stranger smiled, and his heart rate accelerated again.

'Thanks so much. You're a lifesaver.' She rattled off her number and he typed in the digits, sending the photo via text.

'My name's Essie, by the way.' She held out her hand—delicate; smooth-skinned; short nails painted purple.

He shook it, the brief slide of palm-to-palm grating in its formality after the mild flirtatious banter bouncing between them.

'Ash.'

She grinned as if he'd confessed his name began with HRH and he'd come to invite her back to the palace for afternoon tea.

'So, Ash the American tourist...' She had her photo, but she wasn't leaving. In fact, she was twirling that hair again, her eyes glinting with an unmistakable interest—one matched in him. No, his instincts were spot on.

'So, Essie, English fun facts expert...'

Another laugh that shot straight to his balls. 'Wanna grab lunch?' she said. 'I don't know this part of London well, but there's a cute deli not far from here and I have tons more facts about the city...' Her pretty blue eyes gleamed.

Heat soared in his chest. She *was* coming on to him in a subtle, fetching way he found way more enticing than the overt advances of his usual hook-ups. Absolutely, he'd be up for a no-strings one-time with this beautiful stranger. And as a tourist, he needn't spin his usual spiel about *having a good time*, *keeping things casual*, *hooking up* and other euphemisms that let the women he bedded know exactly where they stood. Where *he* stood.

She'd leave London to go back to whatever charming part of the UK she came from and, as far as she'd know, he'd go back to America.

He held out his arm, indicating she take the path ahead of them before tucking both his hands in the front pockets of his jeans. She smiled, swung her hair over her shoulder and set off at his side. For a few beats they walked in silence, the warm summer air heavy with possibility and an insistent flicker of sexual chemistry.

Something stirred in his gut—that delicious coil of excitement that the anonymity of meeting a stranger in a foreign place brought. Today he could be anyone. There were endless possibilities to reinvent himself and shake off the recently acquired shackles that held him down as if his feet were entombed in concrete.

Not Ash the duped, who'd not only been cheated on but also lied to by the two people in his life who should have had his back. *Yeah, fuck that guy.* He was Ash the American tourist, killing time with the interesting, beautiful breath of fresh air that was Essie.

'So...' he flashed his first genuine smile her way, enjoying the telling pink flush of her cheeks '...tell me about these noses.'

Essie Newbold laughed and bumped shoulders with the sexy American she'd spent the afternoon and evening with. Well, she would have bumped shoulders with him if he weren't so tall—instead, her shoulder bumped his arm. But the effect was the same.

Contact.

Those delicious little trembles of static electricity zinged to all her highly attuned erogenous zones as they'd been doing all day, every time their arms had brushed as they'd hunted the Seven Noses of Soho or when they were squeezed together, chest to chest, on the standing-room-only Tube. She'd never been more grateful for the crowding of London's underground.

Instead of allowing the momentum of her flirty little shoulder bump to ping her away from him, Ash scooped his arm around her waist and grinned down at her.

Her head swam.

She was really going to do this—sleep with the dreamy man she'd met in the park this morning? Her first one-night stand.

Essie slipped her hand into the back pocket of his jeans, her fingers pressing into his tightly toned backside. Where had her uncharacteristic bravery come from? The desire for something more than the dribs and drabs she'd tolerated from her no-good ex?

Her ex's idea of foreplay had been a mandatory squeeze of the boob. And to her shame, she'd accepted such lazy, shoddy attention.

All the more reason to explore a one-night stand with the drool-worthy, confident American. She'd gain some much-needed experience in the one-night-stand stakes, and hopefully score herself the kind of orgasm that only existed in her world as a mythical will-o'-the-wisp, and afterwards they'd move on having both had a good time. Unless Ash was a serial killer, it was a win-win situation. She absorbed the foreign, heady thrill of his big warm body next to hers. Not that it was cold—her shivers originated purely from anticipation.

The best kind of shivers.

She sucked in a stuttering breath—she'd never felt more reckless. And, if she was honest, she also felt a little embarrassed. There was no law that stated that, before her twenty-fifth birthday, she should have experienced at least one night of no-strings sex, but, as she touted herself as something of a relationship expert, didn't she owe it to the readers of her relationship psychology blog to experience what all the fuss was about?

Ash's hand looped around her shoulder. She reached up and clasped his fingers. They grinned at each other, Essie's belly jolting in time with her excitable pulse.

No serious scientist could rely solely on academic theory. She could finally verify her years of extensive research with some cold, hard, scientific data.

Surely he must be able to hear the blood whooshing through her head?

Because in practical terms, what did she really know about relationships, especially the functional kind?

Her face fell at the momentary wobble. Her one serious boyfriend during uni had left her practically swearing off the opposite sex for good on the grounds she clearly couldn't spot a decent relationship candidate if he was stark naked in front of her wearing a *pick me, I'm a safer than houses bet* hat.

A trait she'd inherited from her mother perhaps... The woman had, after all, procreated with Essie's lying, cheating, deserting father and spent many years playing second fiddle to his actual wife, his *real* family.

Not that Essie had known all that back then. She'd simply been a girl who desperately missed her beloved father while he'd worked overseas for long stretches of time. Clearly she and her mother shared a desperate-for-love vibe that usually sent men running.

But Ash wasn't running.

And she wasn't looking for a relationship. Just sex. She'd gleaned from Ash's subtext that, like her, he was only interested in a one-night thing. She shoved the buzzkill thoughts from her mind, focussing on the specimen of manly perfection beside her. Exotic Ash. A gentleman. Funny, intelligent and interested in what she had to say.

So different from her ex, and she'd wasted two years in that flawed relationship.

Her throat tightened.

Perhaps she was ready for a change. It was, after all, the eve of a brand-new chapter of her life—her new job working for her until-recently estranged half-brother began tomorrow. Or perhaps it was just charming, sophisticated, sexy-as-sin Ash with his crinkle-eyed smile, his quick wit and his tales of New York that earned him a place at the top of Essie's bucket list.

Nothing at all to do with his muscular physique and his dark good looks, which were enough to attract smiles and stares everywhere they'd gone today. And she instinctively knew, as if it were stamped on her overworked ovaries, that Ash would be phenomenal between the sheets. High-calibre screaming orgasms—another experience sadly lacking from her rather pathetic repertoire.

But she could still back out of this. Thank Ash for

his company and bid his sexy American butt fare-
well. Her insides twisted while her indecision ping-
ponged inside her skull, releasing an uncharacteristic
verbal catharsis.

'I've never done this before.' She nibbled her lip,
ignored the heat almost suffocating her and raised
her eyes to Ash's.

Now he'd think her some sort of ingénue when really she'd simply tolerated mediocre for far too long.

He turned to face her, drawing her closer with the
arm banded around her waist while his glittering blue
stare danced over her features. 'Okay...'

No judgment. Only the heat she'd seen in his eyes
most of the afternoon.

The sizzle and spark over lunch at the funky deli
had turned into flirting around Piccadilly Circus and
Trafalgar Square, where Essie had provided a 'how
to' tutorial on travelling the Tube. Flirting had turned
to inhibition-lowering drinking at a typical Victorian
Soho pub, where Ash had insisted they sample pints
of tepid real ale, which was strong enough to make
Essie both giggly and bold. Which was probably how
they'd come to their current location—on the pavement outside his hotel, with his arms around her and
her lips tingling to kiss him.

Still she wavered, caught between lust and caution.
She wanted to slap herself. Her doubts, her des-
peration to get it right where her parents had got it so
wrong, hadn't helped her avoid heartache. She'd just
had one bad experience...

Ash didn't have to be the perfect man—he could
be perfect for now, this one night. Then she'd never

see him again. And she could try out her sexually sophisticated legs.

Ash smiled, his blue eyes sparkling with promise and his yummy mouth stretching in a sexy, lopsided way.

Full lips so close.

Warm breath laced with hops.

Shrugging off the last reservation, Essie stood on tiptoes and kissed him, right there in the street where people walked around them. For a second he seemed frozen, his stubble chafing her chin and his lips slightly parted as she feathered the lightest of kisses on his beautiful mouth. And then his hand found the small of her back, pressing her close as he took control, angling his head and orchestrating the slide and thrust of lips and tongues, a thrilling concerto that left her head light and her legs weak.

Wow. The easy-going, considerate gentleman she'd spent the day with had a demanding side. She wanted more. The street snog was so good, her stomach clenched like the final seconds of a free fall, and her heart ricocheted against her ribs.

Ash groaned and pulled back from her kiss, his erection a hard length against her belly. He looked down as if trying to dissect her inner secrets from her irises. 'Not that I'm bothered...' he pushed back a stray wisp of hair from her face '...but I'm intrigued. Why not?'

Essie captured her lip with her teeth, her insecurities rising like bile. What did she want this sexy tourist to know about her poor track record with the opposite sex? Despite her psychology degree and her PhD in human relationships, her own love life, and most of her non-romantic personal relationships, relied heavily on the theory she pored over for her studies and for her beloved blog, one she'd started as an undergraduate as a way to purge her own feelings of abandonment and constant rejection at the hands of her father.

Ash wanted her; the evidence was crystal clear. Why burst the bubble? Yes, she normally avoided picking up hunky strangers in parks. But once he'd cracked his first genuine smile, Ash had relaxed into a fun, smart and entertaining guy. She hadn't confessed she lived in South East London and was soon to graduate from her PhD. She'd merely gone along with his wrong assumption—that she, like him, was a tourist. It added to the mystique, the risqué recklessness currently pounding through her blood and fanning her libido to a blaze.

But they'd never see each other again after tonight. Who better to take off her training wheels with than a sexy stranger, a temporary tourist, soon to be on a plane to a whole other continent?

While Ash fingered the end of her ponytail, waiting, Essie shrugged. 'My male role model growing up was an unreliable, lying shit. It kind of put me off men.' Oversimplified, but true. She'd spent years trying to fit her subpar relationship with her ex into a perfect mould, desperate to have the opposite of her parents' dysfunctional union and determined to flex her psychology muscles and prove she could practise what she preached. But when she'd finally conceded that the emotionally abusive relationship she'd pinned all her hopes on was over, she'd given up on her own happily-ever-after and shelved finding love, preferring instead to focus on helping others with their relationships through her blog.

'I'm a man.'

Wasn't he just? She nodded, stopping short of rolling her eyes back at the solid hard bulk of him pressed against her. 'You are.'

She knew enough about human interactions to know there was more to Ash than the charming backpacker, despite appearances. For a start, he was older than the typical traveller, she guessed early thirties. Although casually dressed in slightly rumpled clothing, he carried himself with that air of command, confidence and authority that was such a turn-on—she practically had drool on her chin. That he was bothering to explore the reasons behind her hesitancy instead of ramming his tongue down her throat or hurrying her inside faster than he could say 'God Save the Queen' was another astounding point in his favour.

But the less she knew about him, the easier it would be to walk away. When she left in the morning, she'd feel satisfied no boundaries had been crossed, no misunderstandings had been created and no feelings had had time to develop.

Mustering every ounce of confidence and female allure, she gripped his biceps and pressed her body closer. 'Are we on the same page?' Her limbs twitched while she waited for his confirmation. What if she'd read him all wrong? What if, like her ex, Ash thought her too clingy? Surely he could appreciate the merits of this—they'd never see each other again.

Ash dipped his head, pressing his mouth to hers once more. 'Totally.' The word buzzed over her tingling lips and then the tip of his tongue dipped inside.

With a surge of lust Essie embraced the kiss, scooping her arms around his neck with renewed enthusiasm.

Please let her be right about his sexual talents.

When she pulled back, breathless, she registered her surroundings. They'd come to a stop outside a rather upmarket hotel in St James's. She looked up at Ash, her eyes round.

'Is this where you're staying?' She'd guessed that he was more than he'd seemed in the park, but wealthy...?

He shrugged, a playful twitch on his lips.

Yes, Ash had offered to pay for her sandwich at lunch, but after she'd insisted on paying for herself, he'd accepted they'd be going Dutch for the rest of the day. He hadn't flashed money around—a definite turn-off for Essie, who had what her flatmate called *money issues*.

He released his grip on her waist and Essie missed his touch instantly. 'I know the owner. I'm only here tonight.' He placed his index finger under her chin and tilted her face up to his. 'Changed your mind? It's okay if you have.'

So considerate.

Her body was still fully on board with spending the night with this ruggedly handsome stranger. And did it matter if he had rich, hotel-owning friends? She wouldn't know him long enough to confess her monetary hang-ups, ones that originated with her absent father, who used affluent bribes and constant gifts as a substitute for investing quality time in his only daughter's life.

A shudder snaked down her spine.

One of the reasons she'd taken a job working for

her half-brother, which began tomorrow, was to start earning some money. Finally, after five years of full-time study, she'd actually be able to support herself rather than take more student loans. Because she'd rather be in debt for the rest of her life than take one penny from her scheming father. She'd never once cashed one of the regular cheques he sent towards her tuition fees. It felt like hush money, and by accepting it she would be condoning what he'd done, to her, to her mother, to his wife and to Ben. She'd rather live on a park bench.

Ash, perhaps interpreting her silence as a change of heart, stepped back half a pace, ending the delicious contact between them and leaving Essie more bereft than the dark turn of her thoughts had done.

'I'm happy to walk you home...or put you in a cab.' He shrugged as if it was no big deal but his stare darkened as he looked down at her, waiting. A stare of longing, one that matched the well of sizzling heat rising up inside her.

Don't spoil what promises to be the best night of your life with your hang-ups.

Essie moved closer, her fingers finding the belt loop of his jeans. She tugged, bringing his chest into contact with hers, scraping her nipples to exquisite, nerve-tingling awareness.

No way would she back out now.

'Are you sure?'

Yes, yes, yes...

At her silent nod, he took her hand, laced his fingers through hers and led her inside the glass and chrome rotating door of the swanky hotel.

Essie hurried after him, his longer strides swiftly

guiding her across the elegant foyer that she was too
turned on to appreciate. Her last thought—how nice
it must be to know someone who owned such a well-
appointed and convenient establishment—fled the
minute the lift door closed and Ash pinned her against
one wall with the stealth and predatory instincts of
a jungle cat.

Essie surrendered to the reckless impulses, so foreign but urgently addictive. She climbed him, her own
instincts set free as her hands tugged his hair and her
mouth found his while her legs encircled his thighs
and she clung to him for dear life.

Every taut inch of him was hard. She knew, under
his slouchy clothes, he'd be sleek and toned and bulg-
ing in all the right places. They broke apart long
enough to hurry from the lift to his room, although she
was so turned on that Essie was certain she'd floated.

He took a key card from his pocket, swiped it
through the reader and stood back so she could enter
first. Essie turned to welcome him as he followed
her inside, her pent-up libido and the fizz of adrenaline in her blood making her embarrassingly eager.
She gave him no time to activate the lights or even
wait until the door had fully closed before she leapt
at him, the air leaving her in a whoosh as he caught
her around the waist and hauled her up to his equally
insatiable mouth.

The chemistry between them practically melted her
body to his as if they'd been welded together.

The kissing, unlike anything she'd known, was so
voracious she whimpered out her pleasure. With dizzying speed, Ash deposited her on the bed, whipped
off her underwear and produced a condom.

Essie panted while he tore at his fly and covered himself, a look of desperate concentration on his face, barely visible in the gloom. This was wild, audacious and thrilling. But then Ash's mouth was back on hers, his fingers stroking her nipple to a peak through her clothing while he pushed slowly inside her, and she lost herself to what she was certain would turn out to be the single best sexual experience of her life to date.

She wasn't wrong. Ash pulled his mouth from hers, yanked his T-shirt over his head and reared back. With her hips gripped in his large hands and her stare locked with the white-hot one he bore down on her, Ash pounded into her again and again.

He was a god—ripped torso, a smattering of dark hair trailing down to his magnificent manhood, which she couldn't see, but which was currently rendering her a speechless bag of raging female hormones. When he scooped her hips with one arm, not losing his rhythm, and slipped his free hand between them and located her clit, her world fractured and a broken cry left her throat as she came, shortly followed by Ash.

Yep—best sex ever.

Go, Essie.

CHAPTER TWO

ESSIE EXITED THE Piccadilly Circus Tube station into glaring sunlight and joined the mass of people heading towards the start of their work week. Stifling a yawn with the back of her hand, she dragged her sunglasses from the top of her head and scoped out another coffee fix. Of course, if she'd had more than three hours' sleep last night, she wouldn't need another dose of caffeine. But she always worked on her blog first thing in the morning when the words flowed freely and the ideas were fresh, and this morning, the morning after the best sex of her life, had been no different.

Ash had kept her up into the early hours with his impressive stamina. After a second round of high calibre, sheet-clawing sex, another life-redefining orgasm, she'd sneaked out of his hotel room, like a sexually enlightened Cinderella, in the early hours while Prince Charming had slept.

She sniggered, scuffing the toe of her Converse on the tiled floor. Yes, it hadn't been her proudest moment—leaving without so much as a 'nice to meet you, thanks for the orgasms'—but that had been the unspoken deal, right? The casual sex secret code. One of the pros. No awkward swapping of numbers, no obsessively checking her phone for his call and no stalking him on social media to confirm his single status.

Of course, in practical terms, she was no expert. But she'd been right—what had occurred with Ash last night far surpassed the commonplace.

Good thing he was leaving the country soon. Sex that good should come with a health warning.

Hazard! You are ten times more likely to develop feelings for this man. Avoid sexual contact at all costs. Danger! Disappointment ahead.

And she'd had enough of that to last a lifetime.

Essie accepted her coffee from the barista, wincing as she set off at a quicker pace into Soho—starting her new job for her brother on a few hours of sleep was not her wisest move.

She sipped her latte and checked her phone for directions, cursing at the time displayed as she hurried along unfamiliar streets to meet Ben at the basement-style club and cocktail bar he'd recently purchased and had just completed renovating.

Of course, she wouldn't have needed the map if she'd scouted the route to her new job yesterday as she'd planned. But the sun had been shining and she'd disembarked the Tube a few stations early to indulge in a pleasant walk in the park. Meeting a sexy stranger hadn't been part of the plan. But she couldn't tell Ben why she'd got...sidetracked.

Essie quickened her pace, holding her coffee out in front of her. Of all the days to be late. And for Ben, too. Her older half-brother, seven years her senior, had taken a chance, offering her a job at his new club. Yes, she'd done some bar work throughout uni, but she'd never held a managerial position. All the same, she had assured him she was capable—she had a PhD, for goodness' sake, well almost, the conferment ceremony only a few weeks away—and she was determined to make the best of the chance to work for her brother.

This was more than a job. Working with him would hopefully lead to a closer relationship than the cordial but unemotional one they currently shared. Not that she blamed Ben for the distance—she had been equally hesitant. Their father had kept *her* existence a secret from his only son, too. They both had some making up for lost time to do.

That was why Essie had grasped at his request to help out, when his current manager had quit unexpectedly, with both eager hands. If she had a career plan, bar work would have no place in it, but the job comprised predominantly night shifts, which protected her dedicated blog-writing time during the day. And until she decided if she was cut out for a stuffy academic position, it provided a perfect stopgap. And the pay Ben had offered was great.

Essie rounded the corner, dodging a steady stream of smartly dressed office workers and frantic stallholders setting up their fresh produce and delicious-smelling street food for Soho's famous, three-hundred-year-old Berwick Street Market.

She stepped off the kerb to dodge a fruit and veg vendor carrying a precarious tower of produce-laden boxes six high, narrowly avoiding a delivery van that screeched to a halt. The coffee sloshed inside the takeaway cup with a violent lurch. A spout of scalding liquid jettisoned from the sip hole in the plastic lid and sprayed the front of Essie's favourite dress, deliberately chosen for her first day at work.

She cursed while a trail of coffee dripped down her cleavage and soaked into her bra. Her eyes stung as she dabbed at the brown stain with her fingers and stepped back onto the pavement, pushing her way back into the hustle of the commuter crowds.

She breathed through her disappointment over the dress, her face forcing a bright smile. Ben wouldn't care how she dressed. Only that she turned up, offered him as much help as she could and became someone he could rely on. And if she hurried, perhaps she could beat Ben and his business partner there and she could clean up before making a good impression.

This part of Soho housed an array of trendy bars, eclectic restaurants and small, elegant hotels. The innocuous, black-painted street frontage of The Yard—sandwiched between a designer menswear store and an Italian deli—meant Essie almost walked straight past. If it hadn't been for a van parked on half of the pavement and the sign writer blocking the other half with his ladder while he worked on the shiny new nameplate, she might have missed her destination completely.

Essie followed the harassed sign writer's directions to the narrow alleyway between the deli and the club that led to the rear entrance of The Yard. Yanking open the ancient, squeaky door, she entered the cool gloom of the darkened interior.

'Ben?'

She made her way along a maze of dimly lit corridors, following the sounds of activity, her insides a

flurry of twisting energy, one she couldn't blame on
the barely tasted coffee.

The bar area swarmed with electricians rigging
reams and reams of neon lights into every available
nook and cranny. The sharp chemical tang of new
paint filled the air and a very harassed-looking Ben
paced near the front entrance door with his mobile
phone glued to the side of his head. When he saw
Essie, he visibly sagged and quickly ended his call.

'I am *so* glad to see you.' He gripped her elbows
and kissed her cheek, a gesture that felt far from natural. She forced her breathing to deepen so she didn't
pass out from excitement.

Baby steps.

Although they'd known of each other's existence
for some years, their sibling relationship held a new
and fragile quality. Recalling the first time Ben had
made contact still held the power to suffocate her with
emotions; the date, time and what she'd been wearing
when his call had come in engraved on her memory
as if it were yesterday.

Twelve months ago, he'd relocated full-time to London, which had taken their contact from the occasional
awkward video call to an actual face-to-face meeting. From that moment Essie had been secretly and
cautiously smitten, because all they'd really shared to
date was a genetic bond with their devious and un-
scrupulous father, a string of hesitant emails and a few
quick, stilted coffee dates. If they were going to have
a lasting relationship in the future, using this opportunity to get to know each other better was crucial.

Essie shrugged off her doubts by rummaging in her
backpack for her notebook and a pen. She was here to

lighten Ben's burden. To show him who *she* was. To build on their sibling status, having been denied that opportunity all their lives by their father.

She bit down hard on her lip—she wouldn't spoil her first day by thinking of Frank Newbold. She flipped open the notebook, pen poised, a picture, she hoped, of cool, unfrazzled competence. The coffee stain notwithstanding.

'Tell me what you need. You look stressed.' And so much like their father, a man whose face she could no longer bear to look at.

Ben scrubbed his fingers through his already messy hair.

'The shit's hit the fan with one of my New York clubs...' He winced.

As well as renovating The Yard in Soho, Ben owned and managed a string of clubs in New York, where he'd grown up.

'You don't need to hear my work woes.' His wince turned into a hesitant smile. 'But I am going to have to leave you to things here—I have to fly to the States tonight and sort shit out.'

Essie rolled her shoulders back. That he would trust her with his shiny new cocktail bar and nightclub gave her shivers that bubbled up at the back of her throat, threatening to close off her windpipe.

'Of course.' She swallowed, eager for another of his grateful smiles. 'That's why I'm here.' She could pull a pint from her years of working the uni bar, and the rest she'd learn on the job while her own career path loitered in an uncertain slump. Her motivations were more about personal bridge-building than flexing her managerial muscles in the hospitality industry. But looking at the furrows in Ben's brow and the dark circles around his tired eyes, she knew she'd walk a path of hot coals to help, even if it took her away from developing her relationship blog full-time, one of the ideas she'd considered now that she'd finished her PhD.

A small frown settled between his brows. 'Are you sure you can spare the time? Shouldn't you be job-hunting or schmoozing professors?'

Essie snorted a nervous laugh. Now that she'd finished her PhD, an academic position held far less appeal than it should. She'd considered a university teaching post but was way too intimidated to believe she had anything useful to teach others. She'd love to focus full-time on promoting her blog to wider audiences, but part of her secretly baulked at dedicating all her energy to making it a success—the 'lost little girl' part of her who missed her dad and couldn't understand why he spent so much time away. After all, what did she know about healthy human relationships? Everyone would see through her, know she was a fraud.

'I'll be fine until you can replace me with someone better qualified.' She had plenty of time to build her own career, whatever that looked like. She only had one brother. And, for now, he needed her.

He cracked a wide smile. 'Great.'

Essie flicked through her notebook to hide the attack of rapid blinking. She'd be the best bloody bar manager he'd ever seen. He wouldn't be able to resist falling deeply in sibling love with her.

'So, to recap on our previous conversation...' She tapped the pen on the page, tempted to push it behind her ear to inspire greater confidence. Perhaps she should have bought a clipboard. 'My predecessor has already hired waitstaff, bulk ordered the beverages and organised a cleaning crew...'

Ben nodded. 'All you have to do is be around to supervise things here.' He squeezed her arm. 'You are awesome.'

Warm treacle flooded her veins but she shrugged off his praise with a small shake of her head. She wished she'd recorded the moment so she could play it back to herself in the privacy of her flat later or every time her bones rattled with insecurities.

'The decorators have finished downstairs in the basement, and the interior designer will be here in—' he checked his Rolex '—thirty minutes. Can you make sure they install the leather seats in the VIP area and remind them we decided on the black privacy curtains for the booths instead of the white?'

Essie nodded, scribbling a quick note as they walked. Ben ushered her out of the path of a man in paint-speckled overalls hefting a ladder on one shoulder and offered a tight, apologetic smile.

'Oh, and can you remind the electricians before they leave to install the string lights upstairs on the roof garden?' He sighed. 'Sorry. It's a lot.'

Essie shook her head. 'Not at all. I have a list.' She brandished her notebook with a reassuring grin.

A small nod. 'Have you...had any contact from... Frank?' Ben shot Essie a cautious look, tinged with the usual flash of guilt. He felt somehow responsible for their father's actions, but they'd both been victims of the lies.

She shook her head. The last thing she wanted to discuss was their father and the endless sob story he'd made of her young life. How he'd decimated her childhood adoration of him, a daughter-father rite of passage, through cowardly evasion and cruel deceit. Essie had learned early on, by the amount of time he'd spent in London, that she'd ranked pretty low on her father's list of priorities. But to discover, on her fifteenth birthday, that her whole life, her very existence, had been a lie, that she hadn't mattered enough, that she had a half-brother...

She swallowed back the familiar burn in her throat and shoved her father from her mind. Today was the start of something new, something positive—she wouldn't let him tarnish it the way he'd managed to tarnish every other significant moment in her life. Birthdays, school awards ceremonies, her first prom night—he'd been conspicuously absent.

Ben led the way to a door beside the bar. 'Come and meet my buddy.'

Her mouth twitched with a small, indulgent smile. Despite growing up in Manhattan, his mother's hometown, he'd lived in London for a year. His accent and his choice of slang wavered wildly between the two, something else about her big brother Essie found endlessly endearing.

How could this amazing man be related to Frank? Not that she was the best judge of character. She'd idolised their father growing up, but he'd used his frequent business travel to successfully navigate his deceptions and conduct two separate lives on two separate continents; conceal two separate families.

Essie tossed her coffee cup in a black bag and ducked through the door Ben held open for her.

'Although he's supposed to be a silent partner, he's

up to speed with everything so, between the two of you, you should have most things covered. I'll be back in a few days—plenty of time for us to put the finishing touches to the launch party.'

'I promise, your club is in good hands.'

They'd chosen the perfect trendy and glamorous location—this part of London was always buzzing with young, beautiful people. And now she'd seen the club's interior, which was tasteful, chic and oozing sophistication, that she could participate in her brother's venture filled her with pride and renewed hope. And something less tangible…a small bud, blooming open, affording a glimpse of the full beauty to come.

Belonging.

Something she'd craved for as long as she could remember.

As the door from the bar closed behind them the noise levels dropped as if they'd entered a vacuum. Ben grinned at her impressed expression.

'State-of-the-art soundproofing. Costs a bloody fortune but worth it.' He took a left turn, pointing out the salient landmarks as he strode ahead.

'Kitchen here and staff break room. Staff toilets on the right.' Another left turn. 'You can use this office.' He paused outside a room where the furniture had been sited but still wore its protective Bubble Wrap clothing. He flashed his handsome, lopsided smile and Essie nodded, eyeing the sparse space.

They'd arrived at the last room. Ben rapped lightly on the door.

'Come in,' a voice said.

If she hadn't been so dazzled by the warmth and camaraderie of her brother's welcome and the affectionate bonding moment of him sharing his shiny new club with her, she might have clued on sooner. But she followed him into the room, blind to everything but Ben and blissfully oblivious to the impending catastrophic confrontation.

And came face-to-face with Ash.

The smile she held on her face morphed into a frozen grimace. Her cheeks twitched with the effort of keeping it there, like a painted-on clown smirk.

She scoured her gaze over his height and breadth, seeking confirmation. But, no, it was definitely him.

The verification came, a breath-stealing blow to the solar plexus.

'Essie, this is Ash Jacob, my oldest friend and now business partner. Ash, my little sister, Essie Newbold.'

Essie wanted to run a lap of honour at hearing Ben's description of her, but her stiff skeleton could barely manage a small chin tilt in Ash's general direction as her neck muscles seized like a rusty gate.

Confident, commanding Ash stood, smoothing down his graphite tie as he rounded the sleek, modern desk and strode into her personal space with his hand outstretched in greeting as if he had not a care in the world. Saliva pooled in her mouth, her throat too tight to allow it passage. Her mind ping-ponged inside her skull, playing catch-up.

His gorgeous face, now clean-shaven to reveal a chiselled jaw and sinful creases that bracketed his full mouth, was relaxed, a small, polite smile on his lips as if he welcomed a total stranger, not the woman he'd come inside last night with a yell she heard every time she closed her eyes.

The memory of his now absent stubble scraping

across her nipples gave her an acute pang of longing to see the relaxed, playful Ash of last night. Tourist Ash. Not this tie-wearing, professional version with distant, accusatory eyes and a tense jaw. But for the embers flickering in his navy stare, she'd almost have believed she'd concocted last night's torrid one-night stand. But her hips and thighs still bore the ghostly imprints of his fingertips as he'd held her tight and drilled into her with fierce determination.

'Nice to meet you.' The rich, dark rumble of his voice scraped her eardrums. Her coffee soured in her stomach. How could he maintain such a poker face? Why didn't he suffer the same jaw-dropping disbelief currently rendering *her* speechless? And why, oh, why out of all the men in the universe had she chosen her half-brother's best friend and business partner for her first one-night stand?

Ash's warm hand enclosed hers, reminding her of last night's touches. Touches that should have been more intimate but paled against this simple handshake, because this time all pretence was stripped away.

Ash Jacob was The Yard's co-investor.

Ben's silent business partner.

Ben's billionaire friend from uni. A man she'd wrongly assumed was a tourist and picked up in St James's Park. A man she'd had sex with, twice, whose bed she'd only left mere hours ago. A man to whom she'd confessed her pathetic lack of sexual experience, and thought she'd never see again.

Molten heat engulfed Essie's throat. She swallowed it down with a sour chaser of you've-only-got-yourself-to-blame. But her stomach rebelled the dose of self-inflicted medicine.

Pulling herself up, she levelled her best cold stare on his sinful good looks and returned his handshake with an overly firm one of her own, ignoring the delicious glide of his callused palm.

Social pleasantries complete, she yanked her hand from his as if he were a live wire, connected to the mains.

He'd lied to her.

Deceived her.

Pried into her sordid hang-ups about her crappy father figure.

Why had she told him such personal information? Why hadn't she asked more about him? She really was a one-night-stand rookie. Her burning eyes darted away, but not before his image branded her retinas.

She'd wanted to experience the casual sex hype, desperate to lend an air of real experience and authority to the relationship advice she touted on her blog. All because, despite her qualifications, despite years of academic research, despite actually having had a long-term relationship, she feared herself an imposter.

Of course, the fact she'd been starved of earth-shattering orgasms during that relationship and that Ash was…easy on the eye had helped…

She snatched another scan of his sublime body. Unlike the relaxed, slightly crumpled hottie she'd met yesterday, today Ash wore a crisp white shirt with the sleeves rolled up to the elbows and sharply tailored suit trousers that complemented the silver-grey tie and highlighted the intense blue of his eyes.

Gorgeous. Mouth-watering. A duplicitous scumbag…

As hot as he'd looked dressed down in jeans and

a T-shirt, he wore this sharp, professional outfit like a second skin, as he wore the power that oozed from him. As he lived and breathed the air of command and authority that immaculate tailoring afforded. Her breath caught. She could have slapped her own forehead. Another piece of the puzzle slotted home—Ben's new business partner was a top New York attorney... like a character from that TV show, only a hundred times hotter and a thousand times more untouchable.

But she *had* touched.

The seconds stretched.

Awkward seconds. Seconds absent of the expected social niceties. To compensate, Essie blurted the first inane thing to pop into her head.

'So you're Ben's business partner?' *Duh...*

Ash nodded. Slow. Easy. His stare glittering. As if he recognised the turmoil rendering her tongue-tied. And not one hint of regret or embarrassment. Unlike her, who was practically molten with shame.

'Guilty as charged.' His voice carried a bite that had been missing from the deep, hypnotic rumble of the easy-going sightseer. As if he was used to being in control?

And lawyer humour... Really?

'Ben has been talking about you all morning,' he said. 'Of course, he mentioned a while ago he'd recently united with his half-sister, but I'd failed to pay attention to your very pretty name.' His eyes flicked down the front of her dress. To the coffee stain...

Perfect.

Essie fought the temptation to fold her arms across her chest and keep on folding herself into a tiny origami Essie. Had Ash told Ben about last night? About how she'd thrown herself at him? How she'd blurted out her inexperience and then eagerly climbed his ripped body? Had he laughed at her? And why was *he* pissed? She'd been the one deceived, duped. Dazzled by his confident charm and his promise of a string-free night to remember. It wasn't as if she'd stalked him here for a repeat performance…

And how much of her sad little tale, her pathetic past, did he know? Had Ben told him all about her sorry past? Had Ash linked the woman confessing her daddy issues before fleeing his bed with Ben's sister?

As if he'd heard her thoughts, he said, 'Imagine my surprise when I heard Ben's sister was to be our new bar manager.'

The trembles turned into jolts. Surely Ben would have said something if he knew. She tensed her muscles to hold herself still. It wouldn't do to show a man like Ash, the real Ash, any weakness. Last night, she'd have run a mile from this powerful, controlled man. She *should* run now. Leave with what was left of her self-esteem intact before Ben clued on and her embarrassment became full-blown.

But leaving her brother in the lurch…? When he needed her help more than ever? Not an option. Not if they were to have a chance at a deep and lasting sibling relationship.

Ben snorted, flicking Ash a friendly but distracted grin.

'Leave it, Jacob. Essie's been a lifesaver, stepping in at the last minute.' Ben rounded the desk and flopped down into the chair Ash had vacated, leaving the two of them alone on the other side of the impressive block of wood.

Essie levelled her stare on Ash. She narrowed her

eyes but kept her voice free of the sarcasm fighting to break free. 'Tell me, have you been in London long? Had a chance to do a little sightseeing perhaps?'

For Ben's sake, she kept the acid from her tone, but Ash shrugged, seemingly indifferent, and Ben looked too engrossed in the screen of his phone to have even heard the vague barb.

Ash moved to an informal seating area in one corner of the office, which was decked out like something from an exclusive gentlemen's club. He held out his arm to offer her a seat and then, when she declined, sank down into the leather, all the while assessing her with his narrowed stare.

'I have managed a tour of the more...exciting highlights the city has to offer.' He quirked a brow, his mouth twisted. He reclined, one arm stretched out along the back of the sofa, thighs spread in that confident, manly way that screamed, *Look at my junk! Oh, wait, you've already experienced it.*

Heat slammed through her, pulsing between her legs with every lurid memory of him inside her last night: his hips slamming into her; his gruff voice commanding her pleasure; his uncompromising control brooking no arguments, even though she'd been one hundred per cent complicit.

Her cheeks warmed. She'd fully embraced the *wham-bam, thank you, ma'am.* She dragged her gaze from his crotch, pressing her lips together so she couldn't lick them. This morning, one night had been enough.

But now, with him looking at her as if he wanted a repeat performance, her body hummed with need, in traitorous, clit-throbbing agreement.

One night *hadn't* been enough.

Not of this man, who she suspected would be twice the lover of relaxed, tourist Ash. Was that even possible? No. She didn't want to know.

'So you have managerial experience? Hospitality experience?' Ash flicked his eyes over her from head to toe as if they were alone, his tone grating and transforming her buzz of arousal to one of irritation. It was the way he asked, as if he already knew the answer and found her...lacking.

Another lawyer trait? Or pure, unadulterated arsehole?

Essie changed her mind. Selecting the chair opposite him, she faced him, forcing her body into as relaxed a demeanour as he displayed. She was, after all, an expert at body language.

'I'm a graduate.' She lifted her chin. 'I've just completed a PhD and I have lots of hospitality experience.' So she didn't have a Harvard law degree, but she wasn't an imbecile. She could work a till and wipe down tables. 'Would you like to see my CV?' She pursed her lips in a tight, sickly smile.

'What's with the third degree?' Ben joined them, taking the second armchair. He shot Ash a curious glare and then turned to Essie. 'Forgive my friend. He's not long arrived from New York. He's not used to your English customs and manners yet.'

Ben turned back to a smiling, completely unfazed Ash.

'Look, it sucks balls that I have to leave today, but I expect you to look out for my sister, Jacob. Employ a dash of that charm that gets you endlessly laid.' Ben's grin dropped. A frown lodged between his brows. 'But keep your hands off my sister.'

A titter of hysterical laughter clogged Essie's throat

while her cheeks flamed. She'd already sampled his friend's goods. She lifted her chin, her stare honed on Ash. She might not be able to control her flush response, but she could certainly control her misguided libido.

'I can manage anything your friend can dish out, Ben. Don't worry.'

Both men looked at her as if inspecting her for the first time. Their faces were unreadable and likely concealed very different thoughts. Essie examined her fingernails and tried to keep her feet still.

Although certain she lacked the sophistication of the New York babes Ash probably usually bedded, Essie wasn't a pushover. And this job was about her and Ben. Not her and Ash. So she'd let some personal baggage escape last night, been indiscreet about her track record—that ended right here, right now. Arrogant Ash had seen all he was going to see of unguarded, easy-going Essie.

She returned Ash's stare, the standoff a game of wills.

'Good,' said Ben. 'Because Ash here has a bit of a reputation with the ladies…if you know what I mean.' He winked at Essie, who tried to catalogue the sparse contents of her fridge to stop another telltale blush giving her away.

'Don't worry.' Ash's lip curled. 'Little sisters aren't my type.'

Essie concealed her indrawn gasp with a nervous chuckle. Was he daring her? Goading her to out them to a clueless Ben? White-hot fire replaced her blood— she'd been his type less than twelve hours ago when he hadn't even bothered to fully strip either of them before he'd lowered her to the bed and pushed his delicious dick inside her.

No.

Not delicious. Wrong. Forbidden. And probably as devious as the rest of him.

She cringed, her fatigue-weakened body veering towards kissing the smirk from Ash Jacob's handsome face one minute and coming clean to Ben the next.

Day one on the job, and already locking horns with the co-owner, who now knew more about her than most people…as well as sneaking round behind her brother's back?

Well, from now on she'd be the consummate professional and just get the job done. She couldn't risk disappointing Ben or she'd be back to square one.

Alone.

Rejected.

No relationship with her father to speak of, and no relationship with Ben.

Her whole life, she'd felt somehow responsible for the choices her father had made, as if she were the reason he'd stayed away. And now she was responsible for the mess she'd made of this, too.

But she refused to play into Ash's sexy hands. Her sister status meant more to her than point scoring over Ash. She could ignore him at work, pretend she'd never met him, try to forget how he'd expertly shunted her into not one, but the two best orgasms of her life. She could pretend just looking at him radiating the kind of self-assurance born of supreme confidence wasn't a real fucking turn-on…

Ben's phone chirruped a text alert and he pulled it from his pocket with a sigh.

'My car's here. I have to go.' He stood, and Essie and Ash followed. He stooped to kiss Essie's cheek again and turned to shake hands and shoulder bump with Ash.

'Play nice.' Ben levelled an index finger at his friend, who shrugged, his expression all laid-back charm and cocksure nonchalance.

Ben turned back to Essie.

'And if you need me, email.'

Essie nodded, more than half tempted to fling herself at her brother's Oxford-clad feet, wrap her arms around his knees and beg him to stay. To mediate between her and Ash. To stop Essie from orchestrating a rerun of last night's recklessness. To see that underneath the stained dress and the bad decisions, she was a worthy sister.

But instead she stood and watched him leave while her stomach flopped to her coffee-speckled shoes.

Get a grip. You're a grown-ass woman. Soon to be Dr Essie Newbold, psychologist and relationship guru. Not some insecure sad sack ruled by her hormones.

She straightened her spine and prepared to follow Ben's lead and leave the room that shrank the minute she and Ash were alone, compressing the available oxygen.

'Well, you failed to mention this last night...'

She yanked her stare back to Ash.

Every minute hair on her body stood to attention. Ben seemed to have taken the sun with him, too, because the room's temperature plummeted as Essie and Ash faced off.

'Me?' Was he for real? 'What about you?' Playing

the charming tourist and allowing her to believe he'd be leaving town in a few days. Laughing at her London anecdotes and listening intently when she'd offered top tips for surviving the capital, when all the time he probably knew the city better than her. If she'd known last night that he owned a sizeable chunk of St James's, she might have put two and two together and kept her knees and her mouth shut.

And now she and Mr Moneybags had to survive an intolerable working relationship, where every time they crossed paths she'd blush beet red at her folly.

Her phone vibrated in her bag, a reminder it was time to publish the blog post she'd drafted that morning. Oh, the irony. She'd waxed lyrical about casual sex, clutching her shiny new members' badge to the one-night-stand club. Now the pieces of that newfound air of authority lay scattered around her two left feet.

Perhaps she could quickly pen an alternative piece: *How to work with people you want to...jump.*

No.

Not jump. Ignore.

Ash stepped close, his big manly body producing enough heat to scorch her bare arms, lobster red. Flicks of blue flame danced in his eyes.

'I didn't conceal anything. I just didn't mention anything personal.'

The unspoken hovered in the air... *Unlike you.*

Essie wanted to curl in on herself, but she held her head high. Being eager to take off her casual sex training wheels was nothing to be ashamed of.

'If you made wrong assumptions, that's your problem,' he bit out. 'And what was with the *"My phone died. Please take a photo for me...*" Why were you playing the tourist? You live here.'

She'd wanted the photo for a future blog post, the wheel symbolic of the spectrum of human emotions and the sun catching the Eye a reflection of hope—a new day. But she couldn't tell him that, couldn't tell him about the blog. Not when her reckless, mind-blowing one night with him was the focus of today's post. When she published it later, this new element of fucked-upness, would give the subject matter even more credence—a cautionary tale of how people concealed what they really were to get what they wanted. To get laid.

The perils of casual sex...

'You're the one who lied. Ash the tourist? From what Ben told me, you own half of London.' *Typical.* She'd inherited her bad taste in men from her mother...

She bit the inside of her cheek, scalding heat flooding her body. Her mum was a good person who'd raised Essie virtually single-handedly. No, she only had herself to blame for her foolhardy behaviour last night and its humiliating consequences this morning.

Where were all the honest, dependable, upfront men? And why was she a magnet for the opposite type? The ones who evaded the truth, like Ash. The ones who claimed they wanted a relationship but took more than they gave, like her ex. The ones who made promises and then broke them and threw money at the situation so they avoided dealing with real life, like her unreliable, phoney father...

Ash's stare raked over her features. 'So?' He lifted his chin, looking down his nose with a lazy smirk on his face. 'You didn't seem to care who I was last night. In fact, all you seemed concerned about was marking your one-night-stand card—or was that part of the act, too?' He inched into her personal space, invading until the breadth of his chest eclipsed her field of vision.

Essie placed the flat of her hand between his well-developed pecs, ignoring the burn of his body heat and the clean male scent wafting up from his expensive shirt.

'I'm not the only one who made wrong assumptions. And I rocked your world last night, counsellor.' Her fingers wanted to curl, to dig, to tug. But she forced them to stay flat. Time to put some boundaries in place. No matter how fantastic their brief, steamy interlude, the after shame currently making her hot and twitchy rendered the high worthless. Another important post–casual sex lesson she could impart to her readers.

His mouth kicked up on one side, and he snorted a soft gust of air.

'Funny, I thought I'd rocked *your* world?'

Her internal muscles clenched at the memories of his spectacular manhood. She laughed, stepping away from toe-tingling temptation and heading for the door with a shake of her head. There was no chance of damaging this man's ego, but she didn't trust her voice to emerge without the breathiness that made her light-headed.

'No?' His hurled question stopped her in her tracks. 'We could rectify that situation, right now.' He flicked his stare to the uncluttered slab of a desk, his sinful mouth twisted, but his eyes hot.

Challenging?

Essie imagined herself spread there with Ash, determined to prove something, between her thighs. Thighs that loved the idea if the tremble between them was any indication. She instinctively knew that sex with hot lawyer Ash would be twice as intense as sex with hot tourist Ash. No mean feat.

Tempting.

Lying made sense, serving a dual purpose of bringing him down a peg or two and fortifying her own wobbly defences.

'There won't be anything more between us. I'm here for Ben, my *brother*. And, as you'll remember from last night, I don't trust your type.'

His cocky, lopsided smirk lifted her shoulders until they threatened to dislocate.

'You're right, there won't be.' He closed the distance between them, his dismissive stare dipping down the length of her body. 'Ben is my friend, this is my business and I don't trust anyone.'

'Good. So we agree on one thing.' That didn't mean she couldn't toy with him as he toyed with her. Make him crave a repeat performance. One he'd never get to experience. It was childish and vengeful and filled her with white-hot shame. But she longed to cut the arrogant jerk down to size. To claw back some of the dignity her poor choice and shabby vetting had decimated.

He nodded. 'It seems so. I made it clear yesterday— one shot is all you get from me.'

Her back teeth ached as she ground them together. 'What a gent you are. Ladies must be lined up around the block.' She forced his spicy scent from her nose with a short snort.

He raised his dark brows. 'I've never had any complaints. And you didn't walk away unsatisfied.'

She wanted to deny his prowess. To tell him he'd been a lousy lay, but that was one lie too far. Instead she stepped closer, fighting the urge to rub her body against his like a cat. 'As you're so…experienced in the casual sex department, I'm sure you know this.' She looked up at him from beneath her lashes. 'There's a world of difference between mindless fucking and the ultimate connection found during a real, honest human interaction.'

She dropped her head back with a prolonged sigh, feigning a look of utter ecstasy while she ran her fingertips slowly down the length of her exposed throat. She released a breathy moan, her hand coming to rest at the top of her cleavage.

And then she snapped her head up and dropped her arm to her side. Her expression returned to one of mild scorn while power blazed through her nervous system at the sight of lust glittering in his eyes and the tent in the front of his trousers.

'If you've never experienced the latter—' a shrug '—I feel sorry for you.' She smiled her brightest beam. 'Have a good day.'

She turned on her heel and left his office with her burning back ramrod-straight and her belly quivering in time to the soundtrack of *When Harry Met Sally*.

CHAPTER THREE

ESSIE SPENT THE rest of the day holed up in Ben's office answering phone calls, sending emails and hiding from Ash. For all her bravado, her encounter had left her shaken to the core. Not because his confirmation there would be no more sex in their future left her reliving their one night together, over and over until her erogenous zones ached and clamoured for a rerun, but because, burning with righteous indignation, she'd rashly clicked *publish* on that morning's blog post, retitling it *The OMG Pros and One-Night Cons of Casual Sex*, while still reeling from their verbal and sexually charged spat. And now her tongue-in-cheek cautionary tale of her first one-night stand winged its way through cyberspace to land in the inboxes of the thousands-strong audience her relationship blog attracted.

Stupid.

Reckless.

But providing a belly-warming kick of satisfaction.

Her small, naughty smile turned into a lip nibble.

Thinking about her blog should have brought her a sense of pride. Her usual posts were heavily theoretical and science based, calling on the latest psychological research on relationships, love and the complexities of all forms of human interaction.

But crammed full of shame, betrayal and an overwhelming head spin of good sex hormones, she'd thrown caution to the wind and edited her earlier draft with personal details of her explosive but reckless night with Ash, detailing a pared-down version of the sheet-clawing sexploits and their disastrous morning-after fallout as reasons for prudence.

She'd kept it totally anonymous, only referring to Ash as *Illegally Hot*, but she shouldn't have mentioned him at all. She was a professional with a serious academic reputation to consider, not some kiss-and-tell reality blogger.

Her belly twisted even as her breathing accelerated, a sickening swirl of opposing emotions. The added personal anecdotes afforded her writing an air of authority she'd never before believed she possessed. As if, overnight, she'd become a true expert, at least on her chosen topic.

Heady stuff.

She grinned, dragging her lip back under her teeth as the first comment came in, lighting up her phone with a ping.

Well, BatS*#tCrazy liked it. They'd even asked where they could find *Illegally Hot*…

Bugger—it was too late now for regrets.

She slammed her laptop shut with screen-cracking force. Ash didn't strike her as an avid pop psychology reader—he'd never know.

As the triumphant head rush dwindled, the lip-gnawing insecurity returned, full-blown. She'd begun her blog, *Relationships and Other Science Experi-*

ments, as a first-year psychology undergraduate. Still struggling with the knowledge of her father's betrayal, emotionally and geographically isolated from a half-brother she'd never met and angry with her father's desertion and the lies he'd spun to cover it up, she'd taken to putting her own complex and often over-whelming feelings and thoughts into a sort of online diary. Shortly after, she'd made the mistake of falling in what she'd assumed was love. Two tumultuous years later, the ex she'd pinned all her happily-ever-afters on had left her with her self-esteem in tatters, and her heart seriously doubtful that honest, depend-able men—let alone love—actually existed.

Around the same time, she'd fallen in academic love with social psychology and her fascination with the intricacies of human relationships began, guiding both her writing and her choice of PhD study.

Initially, she'd been amazed to acquire a handful of keen followers who had warmed to her quirky, often humorous take on the complexities of interpersonal dealings. No subject was taboo. From the rude man on the Tube to the day-to-day social minefield of under-graduate life, she tackled the full gamut of complex interactions humans faced and presented the science behind them.

And now she had a whole heap more fodder for her writing in the guise of her sexy but arrogant boss, her one night of orgasmic bliss and the awkward, self-inflicted quagmire her temporary job had become.

Essie reopened her laptop, determined to end the day leaving no stone unturned when it came to her responsibilities towards Ben. With tomorrow's to-do list stuck on a virtual sticky note on her desktop, she performed one last check of her emails before heading home.

There was one from Ben's interior designer and another from his PA, asking for her bank account details for payroll. But it was the one from her brother, entitled *A Favour*, that she pounced upon.

Essie
I left some documents in the safe for Ash to sign. I can't get hold of him—suspect he's still jet-lagged and has fallen asleep. Can you please take them around to him and then scan the signatures through to the bank before six p.m.?

PS A spare set of keys to Ash's apartment is also in the safe, in case he's out of it and doesn't hear you knock.

A combination number and address accompanied the request.

Essie dropped her head into her hands, tempted to headbutt the laptop screen and pretend she hadn't read the urgent missive. The last thing she wanted was any further interaction with Ash after last night's reckless abandon and today's humiliating reunion.

Didn't billionaires have teams of lackeys traipsing after them, doffing their caps and facilitating their masters' every whim? Why her?

But Ben would be in the air by now en route to New York. There was no escape. If she kept her head, kept her focus on the goal and not the infuriating, sexy-as-fuck Ash…her mission couldn't fail.

Get in. *Don't have sex with him.*

Acquire a signature. *Don't have sex with him.*

Get out. *Don't have sex with him.*
Simple.

Ash closed his eyes, braced his palms flat on the tile and let the steaming water pound down on his head. Perhaps it would rattle some fucking sense into his brain.

Stupid. Impulsive. Fantastic sex.

He curled one hand into a fist, knuckles bloodless.

He'd moved to London to claw back control of the wrong turn his life had taken, not to embroil himself in another personal shit storm of epic proportions. While he licked his wounds and disentangled his suddenly public personal life, he'd hoped to forge a new path away from Jacob Holdings. A fresh start. Something of his own, untainted by his father.

Sleeping with the intriguing and exotic stranger he'd met in the park had been beyond reckless. He should have vetted her beyond her flirtatious smiles, her sexy laugh and her astounding body. But he'd been charmed by her bubbly, ingenuous personality, so unlike the somewhat cynical sophisticates he normally bedded.

Cynical like him.

And she'd upped the intrigue factor with her hesitant confession of her relative inexperience.

Fuck.

Ash dumped a palmful of shampoo onto his head. But knowing exactly who she was only threw up more questions. If Essie lived in London, why the hell did she need a picture of one of its iconic landmarks? If she had a degree and a PhD, why was bar work so appealing? And what was the deal with her and Ben?

He scrubbed at his scalp, nails punishing. Now, not
only did he have to work with her—fucking eyeball-
scalding torture right there—but he also had to watch
her prance her sexy ass around his club covered in
those flirty little dresses she liked to wear, all the
while keeping his libido under control and his hands
to his damned self.

Screwed.

He rinsed his hair, welcoming the sting as the suds
ran into his eyes.

Not that he'd known it at the time, but sleeping with
Essie had broken one of his life's cardinal, cast-iron,
unbreakable rules: Never screw a mate's sister—the
golden bro code every decent male lived by.

And he was decent. He didn't use people. He didn't
cheat. And he considered the consequences of his actions.

Usually.

Unlike his no-good, lying, asshole father.

His other rule—never more than one night—well,
he hadn't broken that…yet. Although he'd been sorely
tempted in his office earlier.

It was sure as shit going to test every single ounce
of the rigid control he not only prided himself on but
needed like oxygen in order to resist temptation. The
minute she'd walked into his office behind Ben he'd
wanted her again so badly he'd had to think of his
whisker-chinned, sixth-grade music teacher Miss
Lemmon to stave off his boner.

When he'd awoken at four that morning to find her
gone, part of him had sagged back on the pillows with
relief. He'd done his job. Shown her a good time—
actually, a fucking fantastic time.

Yes, she'd understood the unspoken rules, sneaking out of his hotel room in the middle of the night. No number on the nightstand. No scribbled note demanding he call her. No hijacking his cell phone. But the sense of relief had done little to comfort him. A part of him, the part left restless by betrayal and humiliation, the part he'd hoped to leave behind in New York, had coiled like colic in his gut until he'd arisen before the dawn, taken a frigid shower and numbed his mind with several hours of legal work.

Despite walking away from Jacob Holdings, he still had unfinished deals for the family business, one in particular that, as shareholder, he had a personal interest in. No matter how much he might want to throw his father under the bus in retribution, he had his sisters' future inheritance to protect and his mother's share when her divorce from the old bastard was finalised. At least he could atone for causing the split by recommending a hotshot divorce attorney to get his mother a fair slice of the pie. But even drafting a complex and lengthy contract hadn't dragged his mind away from the fascinating Essie.

He sighed, succumbing to the inevitable. Every muscle clenched and his cock thickened. He gave it a couple of lazy tugs as the memory of Essie's whimpers and her cries echoed inside his head…

Ash slammed his eyes open and slapped the tile beside the showerhead. Here he was thinking about the other ways he'd like to fuck her, when there wasn't going to be a next time. There should never have been a first time.

He'd been done with women even before he'd set foot on English soil. Plus she was Ben's sister and now his club's temporary manager. An employee. And, more importantly, someone he couldn't trust.

Perhaps he could fire her? Employ a replacement manager before Ben returned from his trip and say it hadn't worked out with Essie. But Ben, quite rightly, wouldn't tolerate the slight. And if it came out that Ash had fucked his little sister and then fired her for humiliating him, their longstanding friendship wouldn't survive. And right now, Ash needed his friend—the only friend he could be certain hadn't known what his fiancée had really been up to all those years ago.

Her dumping him practically at the altar had left him struggling to trust the opposite sex, but his father's recent revelations and the public backlash had thrown Ash into a tailspin until he no longer knew which way was up and who he could rely upon not to snigger behind his back.

Of course, Ben didn't know the latest twist, the one that had prompted Ash's departure from New York. How the third wheel in his past relationship—the work colleague she'd claimed to have cheated with—had been nothing but a ruse. A decoy to stave off the marriage his ex had no longer wanted and conceal what had really been happening. Ash closed his eyes against his own reflection in the glass. Some things were so shameful they couldn't be shared, no matter how good the friend.

He completed his shower routine with a bitter taste in his mouth. A taste that morphed into the sweetest honey when Essie slipped back into his mind. With her blue eyes blazing and indignation thickening her accent and giving her extra height…he'd wanted to kiss her pinched-with-disapproval mouth and haul her spectacular ass out of his club at the same time.

She'd duped him. And no one duped him any more. He made sure of that in his professional sphere; his uncompromising reputation had become legendary.

And personally…? Fuck, there he was a mess. But he'd get there if it killed him. He'd claw back control, starting with his libido and the temptation threatening to derail him in the shape of Essie Newbold.

Now he had to spend the next two months both avoiding her and checking up on her so she had no opportunity to hoodwink him again. Not to mention hiding the fact he'd fucked her from his best friend, all the while fighting the urge to repeat the mistake.

Hi, Ben, how was New York? You know how I never date? Yeah, you understand why… Well, just FYI, I fucked your shiny new sister and I wouldn't mind having another crack at it, no strings. Hope you don't mind…

For a man who loved the law, loved truth and valued honesty and loyalty, he had certainly waded in some pretty murky waters recently. And it messed with his already reeling head.

He'd thought a satisfying night with the bubbly, curvaceous redhead would soothe his battered pride and redress the balance. But all it had done was land him deeper in the shit and reaffirm his stance on trusting no one.

Slamming out of the fogged-up cubicle, Ash threw a towel over his head and scrubbed at his hair. Looping that one around his damp shoulders, he quickly towelled his legs dry and then wrapped the second towel around his waist.

Just as he'd finished cleaning his teeth, he heard the noise and froze, every sense on high alert.

Someone was inside his apartment.

His SW1 penthouse apartment equipped with state-of-the-art security.

'Um, hello...?' A female voice.

Tossing the towel from around his neck, he strode from his en-suite bathroom, expecting perhaps to find the building manager or the cleaner he'd hired to ready the place for his arrival.

He came to a halt just inside his bedroom.

Essie stood in the doorway, her cheeks flushed as if she'd been running and her mouth hanging open as her stare took a slow, sensual meander over his naked torso. Her hot eyes settled on his groin.

He'd been hard most of the day, thinking about her and their night together. Hard in the shower, tempted to bang one out just to attain a measure of relief from the memory of her tight warmth gripping him. And now here she was. Wide eyes touching every inch of his bare skin, and the hard again parts of him behind the towel.

Her chest lifted and fell with shallow pants, which pushed her luscious, pert breasts in his direction. Having taken her time leisurely touring his body, she met his stare again.

He lifted one brow, lips twitching, tempted to fling off the towel so she could really go to town.

'You wanted something?' Had she come for a do-over? Fuck—that was refreshing.

It wasn't his usual style, but damn if he wasn't seriously considering bending the rules and bending her over. Just to clarify that it had been as ball-emptying as he remembered.

No. He didn't do second times. Clearly his libido was on New York time.

She stuttered back to life. 'I... I... Ben needs you to sign these forms for the bank. He couldn't get hold of you.' A pretty pink flush stained her chest above the neckline of her dress, which still bore this morning's coffee stain. It did nothing to diminish her allure. If anything, it heightened her attractiveness, a sign she was human, clumsy and lacked the vanity to rush home and change.

'I was in the gym and then the shower. How did you get in?' He took the folder from her and tossed it onto the bed. Perhaps he should offer her the use of his washer and dryer...get another glimpse of that phenomenal body.

Wishful thinking, asshole.

The phone in her hand buzzed, and she glanced at it, distracted.

He dropped his towel as if he were alone and strode to the dresser, selecting a fresh pair of black cotton boxers. If she chose to waltz into his home uninvited...

'For goodness' sake—do you have to?'

He shot her a look, the underwear he'd been about to don still dangling from his hand. Why should he be alone in this fierce, futile and, frankly, damned inconvenient attraction? Time to play with her a little.

'Hey, you saunter into my home, uninvited. If you don't want to find a guy naked, I suggest you call or knock first.'

He tugged the boxers on, noting with a slug of satisfaction the way her stare clung to his nakedness until the last second. Or perhaps she was gloating at his steely length, ready for action. But he was only human. She was a beautiful woman with a knockout body—but that didn't mean he'd act on his unconscious reaction to her. Or his conscious thoughts of splaying her over his bed and fucking her out of his system for good.

Her cheeks flamed.

Another buzz of the phone.

Someone was desperate to get hold of her.

'Got a hot date?'

She scowled a death stare at him, dropped the phone into her bag and then fisted her hands on her hips as if she couldn't quite believe his audacity.

Believe away, darling.

'None of your business.' She tossed her head with a haughty lift of her chin, the long swathe of russet hair gliding over her shoulders. How would that gorgeous hair look spread over her naked back as he took her from behind; the tips brushing her rosy nipples as he pinned her to the wall and sank to his knees in front of her; spread out over his stark white bed sheets as he pummelled her up the mattress?

'So first you accuse me of being a liar, and now you break into my home just to give me attitude?' He could live with the latter, but having his integrity questioned pricked at the crude stitches holding him together.

She glared but had the good grace to blush. 'Look. I...I'm sorry about calling you a liar. You didn't actually lie to me. I just... I was gobsmacked to see you again.'

'Apology accepted. And that made two of us.' Ash

moved to his walk-in closet, still visualising all the ways he'd like to make her come.

'But, I didn't break in,' she called after him. 'Ben told me where to find your spare key. And I *did* knock.'

'Ah, yes. Ben. A bit awkward, isn't it?' He selected a black T-shirt and poked his head around the door as he tugged it on, furious that his urge to touch her again was not only still present but seemed to intensify despite the stained dress, reminders of her name-calling and his own rigid rules. Well, if he had to suffer, he wanted answers. 'Tell me, what is a graduate with a PhD doing working behind a bar?' She was too smart for this job to be a career move, unless her degree was in hospitality management.

She bristled, her hip jutted to one side in a move that accentuated her curves and the shapely length of her bare legs. Legs he'd like to sink between... face first.

'I...I'm considering my career options. Ben was left in the lurch, and us working together is a good opportunity to get to know each other better.'

So she had a mission that involved spending time with Ben? Damned inconvenient for him and his raging inner battle, but equally intriguing, forcing her deeper into the crevices of his mind where she'd taken up residence since yesterday. He needed an eviction notice.

Another buzz from her bag. Why didn't she silence the damn thing?

'Why don't you answer that?'

She shook her head. 'It's just some...notifications.' She breathed a long sigh. 'Look, we're all grown-ups.'

She looked at him while she twisted a few strands of her hair the way she had yesterday. Perhaps, like him, her head was saying one thing while her body had ideas on a refresher.

But Ash didn't do regret over relationships any more—been there, done that. Look where he'd ended up after yesterday's lapse in judgment. And he was damned determined not to give in to the unfathomable desire currently dragging at him. A desire to have a second dip in the water.

'It was just a one-night thing. As I told you, unlike you, I'm no expert. But isn't it best to just…move on? Forget it ever happened?'

Was she convincing herself?

And she was right. His head had moved on pretty quickly—he'd trained himself well. But his libido, and his dick in particular, were as keen as mustard. It must be those damn flirty dresses that clung to her gorgeous tits like a second skin. Or her warm cinnamon scent infecting his bedroom. Or that pouty bottom lip her teeth kept tugging on…

'I'm sure it makes sense to you, too. After all, we have to work together.'

He emerged from the closet tugging up his jeans and buttoning the fly, trapping his still-eager dick behind a row of studs. If only he could trap his erotic musings as easily.

'Do we? Couldn't you resign? Tell Ben you've changed your mind?' Yes—remove temptation. She and Ben could get to know each other on their own time. His own sisters drove him crazy sometimes— how much time did they really need to spend together?

There was a small gasp as if he'd suggested abandoning kittens at the roadside. 'I'm not letting Ben down like that.'

'Surely he won't care.'

For a second she paled as if he'd struck a deep, throbbing nerve. 'Why would you say that? What has Ben said?'

Until today he'd never given much thought to Ben's news a year or so back that he had a half-sister in London. Their friendship had stretched over the years as careers took hold, their recent contact limited to a snatched beer after work or a trip to the gym. What was the nature of Ben's relationship with Essie? How close were they and why had she been out of the picture growing up?

One thing was certain: she didn't know Ben well enough to be confident in his reaction to her quitting. Interesting… He shrugged. 'I just mean I can replace you within the hour. No disruption to service.'

Fire shone from her stare. 'Oh, I just bet you could. Well, I'm not disposable and I'm not that easily substituted.' She stalked nearer, shunting his body temperature dangerously high with her teasing scent—summer, cinnamon and all woman. 'I'm not an inconvenience to be sidelined, quietly slinking away as if I don't exist.'

Whoa, where was all that coming from? He had clearly done more than touch a nerve—he'd sawed one in half and poured salt on the cut ends.

Her eyes danced over his crotch and then lifted. 'Couldn't you move back to New York?'

Not until the gossip-feeding frenzy had died down and his personal life was no longer entertainment news, but he wasn't sharing that shit. And why? So that she didn't have to feel embarrassed about over-sharing with her one-night stand? He parried with a step of his own. 'But then what would you stare at?'

'What do you mean?'

'You're practically drooling, sweetheart. I know I was a little wiped out last night, so if you want another crack at it…' He tilted his head towards the massive bed, which dominated the room like an elephant, every muscle tensed in anticipation of finally getting what he craved.

She closed the distance between them, eyes glazed and mouth open as if lust oozed from every pore.

'I'm perfectly capable of separating a meaningless fuck from the work that needs to be done at the club.' Her stare lingered on his mouth.

Was she waiting?

For the pithy reply banked up on his tongue, or another taste? His mind fogged as her proximity, her scent, her heat flooded his blood with the testosterone that had dogged him all day, just knowing she worked in the same building. Close enough to hear her throaty chuckle while she spoke to contractors and the soft humming that accompanied her fingers clacking on her keyboard.

'*My* club.' Time to remind Miss Compartmentalised who steered the ship. 'But are you capable of the work? Ben and I need someone honest, dependable, committed.' Ash ignored the flare that turned her irises to molten metal. He ignored the urgency of his own needs beating at his body until his muscles screamed with inertia. 'Tell me, who are you today?'

Her hands fisted on her hips, a move that tightened

the fabric across her full breasts outlining her erect nipples…begging for his tongue?

'What does that mean?'

'Yesterday a ditsy student tourist, today a competent professional in charge of *my* club? I don't take well to being deceived.' He battled for his legendary control, which he relied on as armour to protect himself. 'I don't trust you. So until I know my club is in safe hands, you and I will be working very closely together. Got that?'

Her stare narrowed but her eyes gleamed with something close to the incandescent flare burning through his veins. Perhaps that was the answer: to fuck this inexplicable chemistry out of their systems; to quench the fire. He'd said it wouldn't happen again, but that was before she'd stormed into his bedroom. Before all her talk about meaningless fucks and moving on. Before she'd drooled over his deliberate nudity and was still mentally stripping him with her hungry, slumberous stare.

Her mouth hung open while said stare burned the flesh from his features. 'I'd never do anything to damage Ben's business—you're just paranoid.' She dropped her bag and fisted her hands on her hips once more.

He inched closer, chest puffed. 'You've got that right. It works well for me these days.'

Her eyes blazed. 'I'm here to help my brother open *his* club. No matter how much you want me gone.' Her breath hitched. 'Unless I hear it from Ben that my services are no longer required, I'm staying, so you'd better get used to the idea.'

She jutted her chin forward, bringing her mouth

only centimetres from his, her breath fanning his face. She looked halfway to orgasm already—panting, flushed, her mouth saying one thing while her body strained in his direction.

Don't touch her.

Back away.

Too late…

In less than a heartbeat she'd pushed her hands into his still-damp hair and dragged his face down. But he'd been on the move himself. He scooped her around the waist and hauled her from the floor. Their mouths clashed and she gave a cry close to a victory wail as she parted her lips under the surge and slide of his ferocious kiss.

All reason fled. Their tongues touched, the thrust and parry of wildness a perfectly matched duel. Her body moulded to his as if they'd been forged side by side. Her passion seemed to enflame the lust that had been simmering in him since she'd swanned into his office this morning—his knees almost buckled. He wasn't alone.

Who was this woman he couldn't resist? Her wilful determination turned him on as much as it pissed him off and her demanding sexuality was…magnificent. His first impressions about her had been dead wrong. Essie fully embraced her sexuality—another fascinating aspect to her complex personality.

Like electricity and water, they sparked off each other. Her hands twisted his hair until he growled. Her greedy mouth sucked on his lips as if she wanted to consume him whole and her thighs clung to his waist as he hoisted her higher to press his steely length against her warm, wet centre, delivering the friction they both seemed to crave.

If he hadn't been staring her down, eye-to-eye, while they consumed each other, his eyes would have rolled back in his head. Her fantastic body aligned with his, her wet heat seeped through the denim covering his thigh as she ground herself there and her nipples poked through the two layers of clothing separating her chest from his.

A fresh surge of blood turned his dick to granite. Yes.

One more time to banish this tigress masquerading as a pussycat from his system and restore his control over the explosive situation. He didn't need to trust her. He just had to fuck her. Just sex. Great sex. One last astounding time.

With one arm now curled around his neck like a vice, her free hand snaked between their bodies to rub him through his jeans before fumbling for the buttons of his fly. She writhed in his arms, all sexy little whimpers and catches of her breath. Fuck, she was a hellcat. Challenging, uninhibited, eager. He'd been doomed from the minute he'd opened his eyes to the sight of her yesterday in the sun-dappled park.

He spread his feet, cementing his balance so he could do a little exploring of his own. Cupping her ass in one hand, Ash delved beneath the hem of her dress with the other. His fingers skimmed her thigh, zeroing in on her to find the source of the warm patch on his jeans—her soaked panties. With their working mouths and challenging stares still locked, he slipped his fingers beyond the cotton and lace.

She was fiery hot and slick against his fingers, and

when he swiped forward and located her clit she broke
free from the kiss with a moan. Her sultry glare—half
fuck you, half *fuck me*—dared him. Spurred him on.
Not that he required the encouragement.

In two strides, he'd deposited her ass on the edge
of his dresser, which, like the rest of his home, was
sleek, minimal and uncluttered. She spread her thighs,
welcoming him into the cradle of space she created
with a tug of his shirt.

While his fingers resumed the slip and slide against
her, his other hand sought her pebbled nipple, strumming through the layers of fabric. But that wasn't
enough for her. She released her grip on his shoulders long enough to unbutton the top few buttons of
her dress and yank both it and her bra down, exposing one pale, creamy shoulder and a perfect, pink-
tipped breast.

Fuck.

He groaned.

Perfection.

He dived to get his mouth on her. *Just one more
taste*. Then he'd stop this madness.

But Essie was having none of that. One hand returned to his hair, her grip punishing and directive
while the other drove him wild by rubbing his erection
through his clothes. Her pert flesh filled his mouth
and he sucked hard, drawing her in deeper and guided
by her continued twisting and tugging on his hair
and her repeated 'yes'es. Her hips shunted against
his hand, as if she was as desperate for her release
as he was.

Just one more time. Until he worked this baffling

urge from his off-kilter system. This time he'd walk away sated, equilibrium restored. Cured.

Pinning her to the furniture with his hips, he pushed two fingers inside her and feathered his thumb over her clit. His mouth returned to hers while his fingers strummed the damp nipple his mouth left behind.

True to the Essie of last night, she clawed his shoulders, her moans growing in frequency and volume.

'Tell me when you're close,' he mumbled against her lips, reluctant to break away from her breathy and frantic kisses.

She nodded, her eyes heavy and her hair a wild tumble around her flushed face. His clothing was practically cutting off his blood supply to his groin. But he couldn't move, couldn't have stopped now if he'd had a gun to his head.

He left her breast long enough to scoop one arm around her hips and shunt her ass to the edge of the dresser, changing the angle of her hips.

She cried out and tore her mouth from his. 'Yes, now... I'm...'

He dived on her exposed nipple once more, laving and lapping like a starving man as his fingers plundered her slickness and his thumb circled her swollen clit.

She detonated, her whole body taut as her orgasm jolted her forward. If he hadn't been there to block her fall the force of it would have tumbled her from the edge of the furniture. Ash kept up the sucking and circling until he'd wrung every spasm from her magnificent, trembling body. Until she pushed at his shoulders instead of clawing at them.

Her head fell forward, resting on his chest. 'Oh, wow…'

The scent of her hair made his eyes roll back. Thank fuck she couldn't see. He recited the most boring legal jargon he could think of to stop himself from burying his nose there and taking a deep, decadent inhalation. He'd fall asleep surrounded by her honeyed scent, just as he had last night…

Fuck.

His blood turned to liquid nitrogen.

What the hell was he doing?

He couldn't trust this woman.

He couldn't trust anyone.

His body turned rigid as reality dawned.

This had disaster written all over it. This business venture was his fresh start—a place no one knew him or his fucked-up family. A place of anonymity to regroup and wrestle back control. Why was he so fascinated in her? Why couldn't he stay away?

He stepped back, tugging his hand from Essie's underwear and avoiding her confused stare. He lowered her to the floor, steadying her by the elbows while she found her balance and righted her debauched clothing.

Too late for gentlemanly heroics now. Not that he claimed to be either. Not any more. That was a fool's game.

He sucked back a swallow that reminded him of all the reasons his head had been right about this illadvised encounter after all. He'd tasted betrayal—a different kind, but it sucked all the same. He was done with trusting the wrong person.

The humiliating scene at the Jacob Holdings offices flashed into his head. On discovering his father had been cheating on his mother, he'd lashed out at the man he'd worked alongside for ten years. He'd expected his old man to bristle, maybe tell him to mind his own business, but he hadn't expected the vile mouthful of home truths he'd received in return.

Fire snaked along his frozen blood vessels, reminding him of the subsequent damage he'd inflicted, especially on the mother he'd been trying to protect.

He turned away, adjusting his rapidly diminishing hard-on, which recoiled at both the bitter memories of his fight with Hal and the reality that he barely knew this woman he couldn't seem to leave alone.

'What? We're done?'

He turned back and offered a single, decisive nod. End it now. With his sanity and dignity intact, his fresh start still tenable and his principles only slightly grubby.

For the longest beat she stared, her expression neutral but her eyes stormy. Wordlessly she skirted him as if he were a shark and walked to his bed. She collected the file he'd tossed there earlier and returned to stand in front of him.

'So, counsellor—' she blatantly eyed the bulge in his jeans '—the defence rests?'

His fingers curled into fists to stop himself from kissing her sassy mouth once more. Pissed at him and flushed from her orgasm, she was even more breathtaking.

He ground his jaw clenched. 'I think it's best.' He'd never needed his attorney poker face more.

She barked a humourless snort. 'Don't worry. I may not be an expert at casual sex, but I am an expert at surviving rejection.'

What the fuck...?

She pressed the file to his chest, holding it there until his hand replaced hers.

'This needs to be scanned by six.' She slid one last look down his torso to his still-hard dick. 'Have a good evening.'

And she left.

CHAPTER FOUR

'EVERYTHING'S FINE,' Essie said to Ben. His partner wanted to replace her as if she were…an inconvenience. She'd thrown herself at a man who'd had the sense to resist. And she had no idea where Ben's head stood and was too scared to ask. Sure, everything was fine.

Essie hunched over the desk and rubbed at a non-existent scratch. Perhaps that was why her joy at his call was diluted. Fear that Ben, too, would agree with Ash and fire her, then disappear from her life as quickly as he'd appeared.

'Are you sure?' said Ben.

She pressed the phone to her face and hoped her brother couldn't hear the blood pounding through her head. She shouldn't be wallowing—she had work to do. 'Of course. The decorators finished up today and I'm meeting your head barman soon.' Ben trusted her with his club, and she wouldn't allow her frenzied attraction to Ash to make waves or damage his business venture.

No. She and Ash were done.

But the years of self-doubt had infected her fresh start with Ben. Every childhood disappointment, every time her father let her down and every cruel taunt from her overcritical ex rattled in her brain until nausea threatened.

Perhaps Ash was right. She should walk away.

No. She wanted a future as part of Ben's life. And their father had already robbed her of a past with her only sibling.

'How are things in New York?' Had he seen their father? Had Frank Newbold asked about her? She shouldn't care, but that little girl part of her, the part that had idolised him, had flown into his outstretched arms every time he'd come home, still craved his attention, even when she'd declared herself done with his toxic brand of parenthood.

'Someone's putting their hand in the cash register.'

Essie gasped. 'Oh, no, Ben. That's terrible.' A slab of guilt settled on her shoulders. Ben needed drama at The Yard as much as she needed another brush-off from Ash.

'I'll sort it out, don't worry. Did the bank get their signature in time?'

Essie's face heated with the reminder of what she'd done last night.

'Yes.' Despite all the reasons not to, despite Ash's obvious ability to resist, she yearned for the full-on repeat performance Ash had denied her yesterday.

He'd wanted her—the physical evidence, thick and hard behind his fly, had been irrefutable. She'd never have guessed a sexually charged man like Ash possessed so much command over his body. Or her so little.

The trust between her and Ash was non-existent. He seemed to think she was some sort of industrial spy out to ruin his investment and she couldn't be sure he wouldn't sack her at any moment, regardless of her relationship to Ben. But she wanted him anyway. Physically. Another new experience for her.

She'd trusted her ex with a blind faith that left her curled into a tight ball. She'd been so desperate to make just one relationship work that she'd ignored the warning signs—the criticisms, the bullying, the control. When he'd finally grown bored and left her on the grounds that she was too clingy, and she'd seen clearly for the first time how dysfunctional the relationship had been, she'd vowed never again to give someone that kind of power.

And she certainly wouldn't give it to Ash.

But, she'd known the minute he'd stepped from his en-suite bathroom, droplets of water dotting his sculpted torso with only the towel and his scowl as a barrier, she'd intended to make good on her plan to seduce him then walk away. A plan that had put the control of their rampant sexual attraction firmly in her hands.

But that chemistry between them had become a magnetised force field drawing her in, and her plan had backfired. She'd seduced him all right, but she'd bungled it. Failed to put a stop to the wild kissing and grinding that had scored her another orgasm, but scored Ash another point on his 'ability to resist her' scale.

'Are you and Ash getting to know each other?' Ben's voice pulled her back from thoughts of Ash's naked body, every inch of him hard and straining...

No.

Ash was getting to know how easily he could turn

her on to the point of spontaneous combustion. How eagerly she surrendered to their physical need that flared to life like a science experiment gone wrong. How her traitorous body succumbed to the pleasure he crafted so effortlessly.

The only positive outcome, aside from the fantastic sex, was that her blog post on one-night stands had been quoted on one of the UK's top online women's magazines and reposted over and over on social media. It seemed people loved *Illegally Hot*. The spike in followers and comments had, only this morning, spurred Essie into publishing another article featuring the panty-melting *Illegally Hot*, entitled *Dares, Disasters and Don't Go Theres*—those relationships we knew were bad for us, but we craved them anyway—drawing on last night's disappointing disaster. As if purging her thoughts, her fears, her doubts in cyberspace would cure her of her irresistible and seemingly one-sided attraction to Ash Jacob.

It was wrong, but she couldn't deny the buzz that the soar of popularity delivered. She'd always considered her blog as something of a hobby, but, with her PhD complete, perhaps the boost in credibility was just what she needed to take herself more seriously as a writer. She could even start running some pay-per-click ads… invite experts in the field to guest blog… She scribbled down some ideas while she zoned back to answering her brother's question. 'Not really.' Apart from Ash's bedroom skills and his considerable control, she knew zilch. A fact her analytical brain tolerated poorly.

'What's his deal? He seems a little…uptight.'

Plus he hated her, wanted to fire her and didn't trust her.

'Has he upset you?' The fact that Ben had protective instincts towards her left her gooey inside. But the only thing she needed protection from was her own reckless libido. The goo turned to brittle concrete.

'No, of course not.' Another lie. Because she *was* upset. Upset that she'd buckled to her searing attraction to the infuriating man, who displayed enough warning signs to send her running. And furious that she couldn't be certain, given half a chance, she wouldn't do it all over again.

'He...he said he doesn't trust people.' What was that about? Just her? Women in general? The entire world?

'He is a bit closed off...' A small sigh.

Closed off? A massive understatement. She'd need a pickaxe to excavate Ash's psyche.

No. Focus on the sex. Control that.

What was she thinking?

No more sex.

Her voice squeezed past strangled vocal cords. 'How are you two friends? You're such a lovely, warm person.' Ben and Ash had known each other a long time. Essie's stomach clenched. She'd gatecrashed a long-standing friendship with her ill-judged fling. But it was over now.

Ben chuckled and then went silent. 'He wasn't always so...uncompromising. It's not my story to tell, but let's just say he was badly hurt by an ex.'

Something they shared in common.

'It's left him with trust issues that make him a bit cynical.'

Cynical. Controlled to the point of snapping.

Of course a broken love affair would be to blame.

Essie knew both first-hand and professionally that only relationships had the emotional power to wreak such long-lasting havoc. The psychologist in her longed to probe Ash's secrets in light of this new clue, her resolve to ignore him stretched paper thin.

The least she could do, for Ben's sake, was try to give the exasperating man the benefit of the doubt professionally while giving him a wide berth personally. Ben deserved better than returning from his business trip to find his partner and his manager at each other's throats.

Perhaps, with a little subtle digging, she could help him deal with whatever held him back. Because if she knew anything, she knew Ash Jacob was on the run from something. Not a crime...more like a battered heart. She knew the signs—she'd spent years seeing them in the mirror. And she preferred to divert attention to other people's dysfunctional relationships than focus on her own.

The idea that Ash might be pining for a lost love left a bad taste in her mouth, one without an explanation. A change of subject. 'I'll have to speak to you some other time. Josh your star barman is due any minute.'

With her hollow assurances echoing in her head, and her mind racing with Ben's cryptic confession, she ended the call to her brother just as a text came in.

Josh had arrived.

Essie rushed to the rear entrance to welcome the twenty-one-year-old classics student. They headed to the bar and were halfway through introductions when Ash joined them without being invited.

Essie froze mid-sentence. Her body zinged from relaxed to nerve-tingling awareness.

Josh was handsome in that trendy, glasses-and-beard kind of way. But the mere presence of Ash in the space—his imposing height, intense, bright blue stare and commanding demeanour—shunted the room temperature to stifling. She couldn't even waft out the pheromones before they had chance to hijack her brain again and enslave her until she started clawing at his sublime suit.

Before she could question his presence, Ash stuck out his hand and introduced himself to Josh. 'I'm Ash Jacob, co-owner.' He flicked a curt nod at Essie and took a seat at the bar. 'Carry on.'

Carry on? Carry on? How was she supposed to do that when the mere sight of him decked out like the sort of lawyer she'd never be able to afford fried all her neuronal impulses not directly relayed to her lady parts and robbed her saliva-making capabilities?

And sitting in on Josh's orientation? He hadn't issued an idle threat or exaggerated last night. He didn't trust her. He intended to watch her every move in case she put a foot wrong and committed some sackable offence. She bristled. As if she'd *ever* do anything to jeopardise her brother's enterprise. Did he think she'd put her hand in the till or help herself to the vodka? *Jerk.*

All her good intentions to make peace with him, to help him, fled. She'd prove to him that, not only was she one hundred per cent invested in this club, but she could employ similar levels of self-restraint to the ones he'd shown.

She was dreaming if she believed they could be

friends—the sexual-attraction barrier loomed in the way like an immovable boulder worthy of Stonehenge. But that didn't mean she had to act on her...urge. Again.

She led Josh behind the bar, seeking inspiration or at least a distraction from the persistent throb between her legs. How could Ash Jacob's brand of sex be so addictive? She'd only had one little taste...one and a half. He was orgasm nicotine and her poor brain's pleasure centres had taken a massive hit. No wonder she was reeling...

'Ben said you have lots of past experience so feel free to set up the bar area as works best for you.' The words squeaked past her constricted throat and she bent to slide a box of spirits out of the way.

Josh chatted away, filling the stilted silence with his relevant work experience and his ideas for making the bar space work.

She barely heard a word. Too aware of Ash scraping his keen eyes over her while his mouth formed a mildly amused smirk.

But, oh, what talent that mouth possessed. He should forget about law—his oral skills were seriously wasted in the boardroom. She'd never been so thoroughly kissed, nibbled, licked... Her nipples chafed against her bra and her legs grew restless, desperate to rub together to ease the ache at their juncture.

Sensing a pause in Josh's speech, Essie forced her mind away from Mr Jacob, orgasm whisperer.

'What about cocktails? Could you create a house cocktail, something unique, associated only with us?' She'd made that last bit up on the spur of the moment.

She seen it done at other clubs, and it matched the philosophy Ben had for The Yard.

Josh answered and Essie busied her hands with straightening a perfectly aligned row of shot glasses as a substitute for drooling over Ash, who'd narrowed his eyes and begun idly rubbing his lower lip with his thumb and forefinger while he listened and observed.

Forget drooling—she was half tempted to see Josh promptly on his way and ride Ash right where he sat. Or drop to her knees, release him from his sophisticated trousers and swallow him whole. Wipe that smug, self-satisfied grin off his face. Show him she could rile him up as easily, effectively and thoroughly as he did her.

No. They'd been there, done that. The sex was over. She'd humiliated herself enough.

Time to focus on her job and on Ben.

That was the relationship that required her energy. A rewarding sibling bond, family, longevity. Something she'd craved her whole life. After all, she'd put her beloved blog, her future career on partial hiatus just to work alongside her brother. And who knew how long he'd stay in London? If he moved back to New York, the opportunity to build family ties, to be a part of each other's daily lives, would be severely compromised.

Her stomach pinched as if she'd sucked one of the lemons sitting on the gleaming bar in a glass bowl. 'Well, I'll leave you to set up and familiarise yourself with everything.'

Josh smiled and started unpacking the box of spirits.

Essie rounded the bar and Ash swivelled on his

bar stool, the creak of leather drawing her attention to him spreading his thighs wider.

Man-spreading?

Staking his claim as the dominant male in the room?

When she looked up from his crotch, he held her gaze, one eyebrow raised in challenge as if he knew the flighty zigzagging of her earlier thoughts and their X-rated bent.

This was impossible. How was she expected to get anything done when he hovered nearby, watching her every move, tying her into sexually frustrated knots with just a quirk of his brow and some male posturing to which her qualifications and knowledge of body language should render her immune?

She turned a sickly sweet smile on Ash. 'Mr Jacob, do you have any questions for Josh?'

'No.' Ash rose to his feet. 'But I will speak with you in my office when you're ready.'

After Ash stalked through the staff door, Essie hovered in the bar area straightening chairs to gain a moment's reprieve from the hormonal maelstrom Ash induced.

With a deep breath she followed him, finding him behind his desk. She left the door open. Her, Ash, enclosed spaces…not happening.

'What the hell was that?' she snapped.

He shrugged, rising slowly from the chair and stalking to a halt mere inches in front of her face.

'What's the problem? I told you, until I'm certain my shiny new business is in safe hands, I'm all over you.'

Essie's eyes mentally rolled back with the fantasy

his words concocted. Him sweaty. Her writhing. More life-redefining orgasms.

Yes, please.

'I can't do my job with you...hovering. And surely you're too busy...preparing briefs or something?' Her unfortunate choice of words forced a rage of heat up her neck—he'd looked astounding yesterday, both in and out of his tight-fitting briefs as he'd strutted around his bedroom, a supreme specimen of rugged maleness. Every inch of him lean and ripped—all smooth golden skin with a dusky sprinkling of dark hair as near to black as the silky mop on his head. No inhibitions and no need for any.

And even though he'd only been partially aroused then, as he'd donned his underwear and jeans, the sight of him had still left her mouth pooling with saliva and her clit throbbing. *Astounding.*

What was wrong with her? She never obsessed over men, physically or emotionally. Well, not since her ex. Essie Newbold, psychologist, would-be relationship expert—at least on paper—was now far too well informed to fall victim to the games played in the name of those relationships. Ash could do all the male posturing he liked—she simply suffered from a bad case of lust. She could control those...urges. Writing about it helped.

'Actually, I have some instructions for you.' His grin widened, eyes turning feral.

She practically choked. 'You...what...?' Her knees wobbled while she imagined the kind of instructions she'd like to hear coming from his mouth.

Strip. Spread your thighs. Bend over...

Stop.

He lifted that one brow. Mocking. Testing. 'You do work here.'

'Yes, but—'

'Good. I want you to go home now and pack an overnight bag. Where do you live?'

Was he for real?

Where the hell was he sending her?

Had he decided to winkle her out from under his nose by stealth? Send her on some fool's errand and insinuate a replacement in her stead behind her back?

'I live in New Cross.' At his blank expression she added, 'South London. Where am I going?' Perhaps he'd decided to work her to death so she would quit. Did he expect her to pull an all-nighter? The Yard wasn't even open yet.

'You're coming with me to Paris. Do you have someone who can pack a bag for you? We leave at six.'

Paris?

With him.

No way.

'I...I have a flatmate. But I'm not going to Paris with you.' The words had barely escaped her mouth when the throb returned between her legs. Twice as ferocious.

Him.

Her.

Alone in the city of love.

Whoa there. Don't get carried away—this is real life, not some fluffy shit you made up for your blog. He's done with you physically and he doesn't trust you. Oh...and you've used his sexual prowess to val- idate your online relationship advice.

Her face flamed. Why *had* she done that?

He smiled, the feline kind of smile that told her he saw too much.

'Worried you won't be able to control yourself?' He closed in. His eyes dipped to her mouth.

Huh, right... The air trapped in Essie's lungs. He was so close, a cloud of heat rose from him, carrying the scent of whatever he'd used in the shower that morning to Essie's nose.

And then he leaned down so his breath tickled her ear and sent tiny muscular spasms skittering down her exposed neck to reawaken her nipples. 'Now who's flattering themselves?' He reared back, his expression hard, serious, uncompromising. All business.

Bastard.

'We have work to do. Didn't Ben mention it?'

She shook her head, her feeble body swaying as the adrenaline dissipated.

'There's a club we wanted to check out. The best in France. Perhaps the best in Europe.'

He slung his hands casually into his trouser pockets so the fabric stretched taut across his groin. Essie dragged her eyes away, desperate now to get away from him so she could regroup and fortify her defences with Ash-proof razor wire and hormone repellent spray.

'I didn't get where I am today by being second best. The Yard is going to be number one. So we're going to go see what the competition is up to.' He tapped the desk with two fingers and then levelled them at her.

'Call your roommate. My driver will collect your bag in—' he checked his watch '—thirty minutes.'

Essie's weak body veered from nuclear meltdown

to hypothermia. Her mind conjured excuses…*no pass-port…an ingrown toenail…an allergy to France.*

How would she survive a trip to Paris with Mr Rigid Control? There would be no way to escape the temptation of him for the hours of travelling time, trapped in a moving vehicle with only his astounding profile, catnip scent and magnetic sex appeal for distraction. Her poor ovaries would shrivel from exhaustion.

She lifted her chin. 'Will I be paid overtime?' She might as well make him suffer financially if he wouldn't be suffering from blue balls, although she doubted her meagre salary would hurt Mr Moneybags too much.

'Of course.'

'Separate hotel rooms?' She might be unable to refuse his reasonable, Ben-sanctioned request, but at least she would be able to escape the lure of lust when the work was over.

His mouth twitched.

'If you like, but surely that horse has bolted…' He shrugged.

Arsehole.

And why was he looking at her as if he remembered every detail of her naked? He'd turned away from her last night, put an end to the mad ride she'd have willingly enjoyed until the end. Perhaps despite his control he was still interested. That would certainly explain the way he looked at her. Her breasts throbbed and her clit tingled.

But where did that leave her and her tattered and grubby good intentions? Perhaps she should even the score; take back control of the physical attraction that showed no signs of abating, for either of them; remind him what he'd turned down. She narrowed her eyes. If she had to survive the extreme sexual frustration of being in his company she should definitely play him at his own game.

Her phone, set to send a notification every time someone commented on her blog, vibrated in her pocket, a timely reminder. *Aren't you already playing him? Writing about him?* Illegally Hot *is a real person.*

She swallowed and forced her thoughts back to ways of avoiding a repeat of yesterday's humiliating rejection. So he'd resisted once. So he wanted to pretend this insane chemistry would disappear. Time to up the ante. Bring out the big guns. Her mind scrabbled through the contents of her underwear drawer for the sexiest lingerie she owned—a treat to herself when she'd graduated with her first-class psychology degree. Some women loved shoes. Essie loved frilly knickers.

At least her roommate, Sarah, would be home cramming for exams today—she'd buy her flatmate something gorgeous from Paris to say thanks. A small smile tugged her mouth. Why should she suffer alone? The least she could do was take him down with her.

'Fine. And I insist on separate rooms.' She moved to the door, halting at his sexy drawl.

'Oh, and, Essie. Don't forget your passport.' With a wink that made a strangled gasp catch in her dry throat, he closed the door behind her.

The car probably cost more than her rented flat in South London—soft leather seats, sleek, shiny bodywork and chauffer driven. It even had a privacy screen. Not that they'd need that. The minute Ash held open the door for her and ushered her inside, he pulled out his phone and began tapping away.

Essie normally enjoyed silence—you could learn a lot about someone by people-watching. Their tells, their habits, their unconscious body language. But all she'd learned about Ash, apart from that the man never looked anything less than seriously fuckable, was that she wanted to know more.

Ben had told her Ash was from New York royalty, his family dating back to a wave of nineteenth-century immigrants. He'd worked for Jacob Holdings, his family-owned real estate business, since leaving college. He'd been to Harvard, and his net worth made her light-headed. But why had he moved to London? Who had broken his heart? And why couldn't he be less attractive so she wasn't incapacitated by the urge to jump him?

'Forgive me.' He looked up from his phone, his deep voice interrupting her train of thought. 'The time zones are messing with my schedule. I had some New York deadlines to meet.' He pocketed the device and gave her his full, panty-melting attention.

Essie shivered, hot then cold, sliding her own phone into her pocket. She almost preferred being ignored.

The device buzzed immediately, halting whatever Ash had been about to say.

'That goes off a lot. Do you have a bet on? Tracking the stock market?' Playful glints sparked in his eyes, but she couldn't enjoy the banter for the slosh of stomach acid burning inside her. Her fans loved *Illegally Hot* and wanted more of him. She knew the feeling.

If only they could see him, edible in his crisp suit, his hair dishevelled and a scruffy smattering of facial hair reminding her how it felt to be kissed by that beautiful mouth.

'Something like that.' She shrugged, her cheeks hot. She should never have started the *Illegally Hot* posts. She changed the subject before she confessed.

'So, this club we're scouting—is there a dress code?' She only owned one little black dress, one she had asked Sarah to pack into her overnight bag. She'd seen plenty of photos of him with hot dates— gorgeous, sophisticated women: models, actresses, heiresses. Compared to the women he usually associated with, she'd definitely be the country mouse.

Except this wasn't a date. It didn't matter what she wore. She should have brought a bin bag, just so her libido stayed in check.

Ash turned and slid his gaze along the length of her body until she squirmed and heat flooded her panties. 'Whatever you wear will be fine.' A shrug. 'I know the owner.'

So it wasn't a date. That didn't mean she couldn't enjoy tormenting him while she suffered right alongside. Regardless of his impressive willpower, he looked at her as if she might as well be naked. His eyes wanted her even if the rest of him could resist.

'You can change on board. We'll be going straight to the club when we land.'

So they were still on the clock? Shame. Now she had him in a chatty mood, she'd like to unearth one or two juicy personal details to fill in the blanks. Like why he'd walked away from his New York life, his family business and what must be an extremely lucrative legal career. And why someone of his social standing, exceptional hotness and phenomenal bedroom skills was still single? No halitosis, in possession of a full head of luxuriant hair, and he wasn't a pervert.

'It's not my area of expertise, but Josh seems competent enough—would you agree?' He rubbed at his bottom lip, drawing her eyes there.

She'd probably agree to anything for the intense stare he settled on her and what it did to her pulse. How was she going to survive this trip when every nerve in her body vibrated, desperate to have him lose that control he wore like a second skin? Lose it with her.

'He does. It's not my area of expertise, either, although I can pull a pint.' Her cheeks warmed. She'd pulled him, too. In a park. She stuttered on, changing the veer of her thoughts. 'The DJ called to speak to Ben—know anything about techno house?'

Ash rubbed his jaw as if his scruff irritated him, and Essie's fingers twitched. That stubble had been amazing scraping across her sensitive nipple last night. How would it feel on her inner thighs?

Oh, no...don't go there.

Her experiences of oral sex were sadly unfulfilling. Her ex had claimed he didn't care for it, although he loved it when she returned the favour. She cringed at her younger self. Of course her ex had lacked skills in the foreplay and stamina departments, too—probably why she was struggling to resist the phenomenal Ash. She knew instinctively he would excel at oral sex— she'd kissed him after all, felt his mouth at her breasts... She discreetly blew at the wisps of hair clinging to her heated forehead. Another dangerous temptation to add to the growing list.

He smiled, the genuine, lopsided version that had landed her in this mess in the first place. 'No, not much. You?'

Essie shook her head. She loved to dance, but her clubbing days were few and far between. Long years of research-laden academic study had put paid to partying and wild nights out. And she hadn't been interested in the hook-up side of clubbing after she'd had her fingers burned with her ex.

'Perhaps we can leave that to Ben, on his return.' He leaned back in the seat and looked out of the window at the passing city, the route to London City Airport taking them parallel to the river. 'So, tell me about you and Ben. You didn't grow up together?' He turned a shrewd stare her way.

Great. So he wanted to make conversation and he'd chosen the one subject that made her skin raw and her scalp prickle. Her relationship with her brother was still so fragile, and brought all her insecurities to the surface like a rash.

Ben and Ash were friends. But Ash had barely heard of her... Was Ben ashamed of the connection with his illegitimate half-sister? Or perhaps she was so low down on his list of priorities... Been there, done that.

She shook her heavy head. 'We share a father, but I grew up here and, as you know, Ben in New York.'

It shouldn't matter that Ben hadn't discussed her with his oldest friend enough for Ash to remember her name. Yes, Ben had been the one to reach out after he'd discovered the truth about Frank Newbold's other life. But perhaps he now regretted the impulse. Did he consider her a cling-on? An inconvenience? Something else to be managed or swept under the carpet?

Could she really blame Ben for being ashamed to broadcast the existence of a sibling he knew little about, his father's sordid secret? The shame she'd felt growing up with Frank's constant absences and see-through excuses rose to the surface, boiling hot. Could she criticise Ben when her own father hadn't found her lovable enough for him to stick around?

She choked down familiar fears. 'What about you and Ben? He said you've been friends since grade school.'

Ash nodded, glancing away. 'He's a good friend.'

Well, that seemed to be the end of that.

'You don't give much away, do you?' The trust issues Ben talked about?

'Try me.' He lifted one brow, daring her.

So tempting. But she didn't want to scare him into brooding silence once more. Something easy. 'Do you have a sister?'

He nodded. 'I have two—twins. Younger. Both a pain in my ass.' He smiled, flashing the grooves around his mouth.

'What about girlfriends? Anyone pining for you back in New York?' Her throat grew hot and achy. Why had she asked that?

'No.' He shrugged. 'I don't do girlfriends.'

'Not ever?'

He shook his head, a slow measured action that gave his stare plenty of time to scrape over her heated face. 'Not for years.'

So the ex hadn't just hurt him, she'd ruined him. He

really was as closed off as she'd suspected. She took pity on the grey tinge to his handsome face. 'Human interpersonal relationships are...complex.' Hers included. All she knew about the opposite sex, beyond the theory she'd got from books and lectures, she'd learned from the behaviour of her selfish, largely absent father and her cruel, manipulative ex. She swallowed down the familiar lump threatening to make her feel two inches tall and changed the subject.

'Fun fact—did you know that having an older sibling can positively improve your mental health?'

He frowned as if she'd spoken in Russian.

She nodded, warming to her favourite subject. 'It... it's been scientifically proven. Ben and I have only connected recently, but...' She shrugged. She hoped it was true. Hoped what she found with Ben would positively impact both their lives for years to come.

His eyes narrowed slightly, as if he were seeing her for the first time. 'So Frank Newbold and your mother had an affair?' His lips formed a grim line, judgment hovering in his stare.

Essie squirmed as the acid in her throat burned its way through her internal organs. She bristled, lashing out instead of curling in on herself. 'Not exactly. Not every relationship is sordid—sometimes people are duped, lied to, manipulated.' The excuses kept on coming, as if she'd waited too long to purge. 'My mother didn't know about Ben and his mother until after I was born. Frank spun her the usual bullshit about having a rocky marriage and leaving his wife when the time was right...' Essie herself hadn't known until her fifteenth birthday. 'By then I was Daddy's little girl and Mum couldn't bear to break my heart with the truth that he'd probably never fully commit to us. I guess she always held out hope that one day we'd be a proper family.' Her throat burned so badly now she was surprised she could speak at all.

'So you didn't know about Ben?'

She sighed and shook her head. 'I was fifteen when I found out.' He stayed silent so she continued. 'My father was overseas, and I was angry that, yet again, he wouldn't be home for my birthday.' The burn invaded her eye sockets. Why tell him this? Speaking the words aloud wouldn't lessen the impact of the events. 'I stayed awake until the middle of the night, crept downstairs and called him at work. He wasn't at the office, but I was given another number I assumed was a hotel. A woman, Ben's mum as it turned out, answered the phone and I said I was his daughter. I'm not sure who was more shocked.'

A disbelieving frown. '*That's* how you discovered you had a brother?' Ash stopped just short of allowing his jaw to drop open.

She nodded, her face flaming. Not a pretty story, and one it seemed, despite his friendship with Ben, he'd never heard. She wasn't surprised. Why would Ben want to advertise such a sordid tale?

Ash's skin took on a green hue, his mouth now a fully blown grim line. Was he that appalled by her tawdry past? How dared he be so…judgmental?

The question stuck in her throat. She ripped it out, needing confirmation. 'Ben…never talked about me?'

He sighed. 'Not much. A mention here and there. But I…was busy…with work stuff at the time.' He grew pensive and turned to look out of the car window again. 'Perhaps if I'd known more about you, we might have avoided this…situation.' He spoke quietly, almost to himself. But the words stung just the same.

So now she was a situation? She wasn't the only one to blame for where they found themselves. 'So you usually screen all the women you sleep with, do you?' That must take up all his spare time, if the reputation Ben hinted at and the pictorial evidence was accurate.

He turned an inscrutable expression on her, but his eyes blazed. 'No. You didn't screen me, either, *your* first one-night stand. Perhaps we should both be a little more selective in future.'

She jutted her chin forward, humiliation making her irrational. 'What, next time you find an obliging stranger in the park?' She couldn't look at him, but she couldn't look away.

'Hey, you came on to me—all I did was make the mistake of sitting in a public place.' He leaned in, hard shards of metal in his stare.

What was wrong with him, making conversation one minute, lashing out the next?

What was wrong with her, digging for answers and then shooting the messenger?

'Well, all *I* did was make the mistake of sleeping with some sort of…Jekyll and Hyde character.' Could his signals be any more mixed? Just like the justifications and excuses currently spinning through her head and making her seasick.

They'd hissed the last few comments to each other, their faces drawing nearer and nearer as they made their respective points. Now, only a couple of centimetres separated them.

His warm breath caressed Essie's parted lips.

Her pants forced her breasts closer and closer to his chest with each breath.

His bold stare dipped to her mouth.

Her fingers curled into the leather upholstery.

She leaned in…

'Sir, we're here,' said the driver.

Essie flopped back, spent. This couldn't go on. They'd never survive sharing a workplace sexually sparking off each other like this, and the minute Ben came back from New York, he'd see straight through them and their barely contained animosity. Perhaps Ash would get his way—perhaps Ben would fire her.

Drastic circumstances called for drastic measures.

Damn, what was a girl to do?

CHAPTER FIVE

'YOU HAVE GOT to be kidding me...' Essie spun on him the minute they boarded the cute little Learjet he'd hired to take them to Paris. Her baby blues flashed and she popped out one hip as she glared in slack-jawed astonishment.

'What do you mean?' He was used to impressing women with his wealth. He'd never experienced whatever snit had worked its way beneath her creamy skin.

She scanned the sumptuous interior, which was starkly white, from the plush carpeting to the soft leather seating.

'All this?' She spread her arms wide to encompass the luxury, her nose wrinkled as if he'd offered her a ride to Paris inside a dumpster. 'Ever heard of global warming? Carbon footprints? Scheduled flights? The Eurostar?'

Was she for real?

He swept past her, loosening his tie and shrugging off his jacket to drape it over one of the wide white leather seats that offended her so much.

'I'll plant a damn forest. Sit down.' Damn, she riled him up. Bubbly and playful one minute, vulnerable and hesitant the next and then hissing and wild when he overstepped some line he couldn't see. His cock stirred for the hundredth time that day. This torture had to end. One way or another.

After she'd left his apartment last night, his balls had been so blue he'd returned to his en-suite, switched the water to arctic and banged one out. Then he'd put out some feelers among his fellow legal professionals in the UK to see if anyone was looking to take on a new partner. As soon as Ben returned, he'd distance himself from the day-to-day running of The Yard. His commitment was always supposed to have been financial, with a spot of legal work thrown in pro bono.

When he'd walked into the bar this morning to see her smiling at Josh, he'd been so desperate to quench his constant need for her, his testosterone-addled mind had considered selling his stake in The Yard just to rid himself of her sunny smile and tinkling laugh, both of which he'd grown to crave as much as burying himself inside her again. What was it about her? And where could he get a shot to render himself immune?

But the more he discovered, unearthing the conundrum that was Essie Newbold as an archaeologist scraped away a layer of ancient dirt, the more he wanted to know. Who was this woman who intrigued him so much?

He had some answers—no wonder working for Ben, despite being overqualified, was so important to her. The need to connect with her brother shone from the vulnerable look in her eyes when she talked about him. And she wasn't secure in their relationship, a fact confirmed by the brittle tetchiness at Ash's clumsy comments.

What the hell had Frank Newbold done to her? Was that what she'd meant when she'd said she was an expert at rejection?

Well, they had an hour—plenty of time to fill in a few more blanks. He waited until she'd settled in the chair opposite his before he selected two glasses from the bar and an ice-cold bottle of white wine and then sat opposite. A small table separated them but it might as well have been a spider's web for all the protection it afforded. And he needed as many obstacles as he could get—the struggle to keep his hands off her grew more urgent every second he spent in her exasperating, but highly addictive, company.

He poured them both a glass while the two-man crew readied the plane for take-off. If he didn't occupy his hands and his mouth somehow, he was going to splay her open and drop to his knees on the plush carpet and taste something other than her sassy mouth.

Carbon footprints...

The car journey alone had been an exercise in extreme gratification avoidance—he deserved a damned medal. He'd never had to work so hard to keep his hands to himself and his dick in his pants. And the novelty had grown pretty thin. An hour's travel time to Paris... An hour of looking but not touching. Fuck, he was more of a mess now than when he'd left New York with his bags packed full of betrayal and indignation and paps nipping at his heels. But the conversation helped—he wanted to know what made her tick almost as much as he wanted to kiss her again and then lay her over this table at thirty thousand feet.

Fuck.

When Ben had suggested Essie accompany him to

Paris, he'd baulked at the idea. But Ben's proposal had made sense. After all, she was their temporary manager. This was the best way to iron out prospective teething problems before the doors opened. They'd only have one shot at making a first impression on the city.

Professionally, everything he touched became a success—The Yard would be no different. He wouldn't allow the failure that dominated his personal life to taint his work. And returning to Jacob Holdings with his tail between his legs after the public row between him and his father in their open-plan office area...not an option. The man was lucky Ash hadn't laid him out.

Ash took a slug of wine, wishing it were Scotch. He needed a distraction from the destructive thoughts and the dangerous urge to lose himself between Essie's magnificent thighs.

'What is your area of expertise?' He picked up the earlier conversational thread. He imagined her doctorate wouldn't be in bar work.

His question startled her—good. If he was to be off balance in her company... 'You said it's not bar work' He licked the wine from his lip and her eyes flared.

Yes.

Those pools of intelligence drew him in—she wanted him, too.

'I have a psychology degree and I've just completed a PhD.'

He frowned. Psychology? Well, that made sense. She was smart. She cared about people. And she could probably spot his bullshit a mile away. His collar tightened a fraction.

And then a fraction more. 'Why did you move from New York?' She jutted her chin in his direction.

Bingo.

He wasn't touching that one. Another millimetre tighter... New York was full of ghosts, full of reminders of his blindness and his failures and his guilt. And full of gossip on the state of his family and his past love life.

While she waited for his answer, Essie took a sip of wine. Her lips caressed the rim of the glass and she hummed her appreciation—blessedly distracting sound that shot straight to his aching balls.

At his prolonged silence she placed the glass on the table and narrowed her eyes. 'So it's okay to pry about my cheating father, my messed-up family, but you can't answer a simple question? Interesting.' She flicked her eyebrows up, her blue stare way too perceptive.

Fuck, the last thing he needed was her probing his head. He threw her a bone. 'Would it appease you to know I have a cheating father, too?' She stared, openmouthed. 'That my sister, Harley, grew up knowing our father had cheated on our mother with an old family friend but only recently confided in the rest of us?'

Ash had been defending Harley and his mother when he'd confronted Hal at the office that day. But all the arrogant Hal Jacob had heard was criticism—something the megalomaniac couldn't tolerate.

Essie's eyes widened as she waited for more. But sharing his sob story wouldn't change the outcome. She wasn't the only one with a crappy father figure.

Discovering his father had cheated on his mother and made Harley complicit in keeping the secret had turned his stomach. But it had been the blows to come that had nailed the coffin lid shut for good on his relationship with a man he'd worked for his whole adult life. A man who was supposed to love him.

Essie leaned forward, placing her hand flat on the table between them as if offering the support of her touch, something he wanted but didn't dare accept. 'Does your mother know? Is that why you don't trust people?'

Ash forced himself to take a slow swallow of wine. Her questions left him raw, reeling, the truth too shameful to speak aloud.

Half the truth. 'She knows.' Ash had been the one to tell her of Hal's final revelation, thrown at his son in a fit of extreme spite during that fateful argument— that Ash's fiancée's affair with one of his co-workers had been a ruse, one big cover-up, to hide the fact that the man she'd been screwing was him, his own father.

'It's okay.' She levelled sombre eyes on him, full of compassion. 'I understand. When someone betrays our trust, we just want to protect ourselves.'

Yes, Ash had battled betrayal. His fiancée had chosen the father over the son. Perhaps she'd hoped Hal would leave his wife. But his father's involvement had shown Ash's whole life to be one big lie. He swallowed the razor blades stuck in his throat.

'Are your parents still together?' Essie's gentle probing continued.

He should change the subject. She'd winkled out the truth as easily as if she'd stripped him naked. But he surprised himself by answering honestly, albeit a truncated version of the final shit storm that had had him walking away from his New York life.

'No.' He couldn't add his part. He hadn't thought the consequences through yet. The public row had been photographed by some Jacob Holdings employee, who'd passed the photos to the gossip rags. Ash had needed to ensure his mother wasn't the last to know.

He fought the urge to shrink down into the leather. His mother hadn't known about the second affair with Ash's fiancée.

He looked away. Intelligent, compassionate Essie saw too much. And the inside of his soul, the hot pool of guilt simmering there, wasn't pretty.

He grabbed a lifeline, any lifeline would do. 'Tell me about your PhD.'

Essie stared him down. She saw through his pathetic deflection technique—had probably learned about the tactic on day one of her psychology degree.

So his personal life had spiralled out of control. He focussed on the chemistry dogging his every interaction with this woman, present even in this quiet, albeit stilted conversation that dragged him too close to the edge of a cliff, but also offered deeper insights into the woman occupying all his thoughts and fantasies.

Was he seriously considering another tumble?

Another shot at distraction with the fascinating Essie?

She released a small sigh through those plump, rosy lips of hers, letting him off the hook. Lips he'd like to see wrapped around his... He discreetly adjusted himself under the table. The abrupt change of tack helped restore his equilibrium.

'I have a PhD in Human Relationships. Just finished it actually.'

Another choking sensation, as if his collar had now shrunk two sizes.

He gaped. Fucking perfect. The one woman who had threatened his one-night rule since he'd created it was some sort of…happily-ever-after guru. Totally understandable after her short-changed parenting from Frank. But Ash wasn't a happily-ever-after guy.

She didn't seem to notice the meltdown passing through his body.

She twirled the stem of her glass while she continued. 'My study looked at the social interactions in modern families in the Western model and compared them to those in other cultures—cultures with multi-generational family bonds, where people live in close proximity to extended family.'

Well, that sounded better—more science, less agony aunt. Ash released some air past his strangulated throat.

'So you're a…' he could barely utter the words '…relationship expert?' Next thing she'd be telling him she wrote one of those advice columns. What the actual fuck had he gotten himself into? And why was he more intrigued than ever? Even this revelation wasn't enough to dampen his need for her, a torture that surely rivalled anything on offer at the London Dungeon.

Instead of the glare he'd expected, she tossed her head back while she laughed a dirty laugh. His body reacted with futile predictability. He'd had first-hand knowledge of the silky soft taste of that neck—the way she moaned louder when he tongued that spot just below her ear.

Her hand clutched her chest. 'Oh…your face.' She grinned and took another sip of wine.

At least her mocking him had snapped all that confessional tension. Thank fuck.

'Don't worry. I'm not trying to trap you into marriage, counsellor.'

'What do you mean?' Was he *that* transparent? Could she see the sweat beading on his top lip? Hear his balls screaming while they ran for the hills? See how close he was to spiralling out of control?

'You have that deer-in-the-headlights look.' Her lip curled. 'Trust me—I know that look well. My father, Ben's father, perfected something similar every time I asked him if he'd make it to my school plays or my birthday parties. Every Christmas that look came out, as predictable as Christmas carols or the Queen's speech.'

She blinked and stared at her wine glass. Ash wished he'd just gone down on her instead of starting a conversation—at least he might have put a smile on her beautiful face.

'He had this look—a sideways glance, a shifty, non-committal murmur...and I knew my celebrations would be a single-parent affair. That I didn't matter to him enough.' Her glassy eyes took on a faraway look. If she cried, he'd be doomed.

But she sniffed and tilted her defiant chin up once more. 'Sorry...it's a bit early for wine.'

What the fuck...? So not only had Frank Newbold strung along two families, kept two women dangling, but he'd also done some serious damage to his daughter's self-esteem. Smart, emotionally intelligent Essie had been constantly let down, left waiting and wondering, probably questioning her worth. Ash sobered. 'I...I'm sorry.'

He'd met her father many times. He hadn't seemed like the piece of work she described, but then, he'd kept his mistress and his daughter a secret from everyone for more than fifteen years.

No wonder Ben hadn't said much on the topic—how did his friend feel about the revelations?

But what did Ash know about fathers? He was clearly an appalling judge of character where his own was concerned. He hadn't been able to see what was happening right under his nose, with the two people who should have loved him most.

So Essie was as messed up as him. Beautiful, intelligent, funny and caring—but probably none of those things in her own eyes.

With a slug of wine, she seemed to compose herself. 'Sorry. You probably got more than you bargained for with that question.'

True. But just meeting her had been a not unwelcome tornado, ripping through his already weather-beaten soul. He wanted to pry further; to offer her words of consolation; to tell her she did matter. That she was all those things and much, much more. Tell her that he understood what it was like to have a shitty, selfish parent. But that would involve opening up his own pain for inspection.

Nope. Not an option.

His hand twitched, seconds from reaching for hers. But if he touched her now, he wouldn't stop until he'd slaked every need burning inside him.

Show some control, man.

She stood, all amusement leached from her pale face after her personal confession. She looked as sick as he felt.

'Look.' She braced her hands on the table so her delectable chest filled his vision, a distraction he indulged in for a dizzying split second.

'I understand you have…issues. Who doesn't? But, this—' she waved her hand between them, as if the constant crackle of sexual tension were a living breathing, visible thing '—isn't going away. I'm not letting my brother down because *you* can't separate sex from business.'

He sputtered, almost choking on his wine. Could she separate the two? A small smile tugged his mouth. It had been a very long time since anyone had surprised him as much as she had. Damn. Another magnificent point in her favour. And bringing talk back to the reason they couldn't stop looking at each other with lusty eyes—genius. Why hadn't he thought of that?

'So, I think we should find a way to work this from our systems.' Reaching for her wine, she took another slug. 'Now, please show me where I can change into something more appropriate for clubbing.'

Change…? No way.

He swept his eyes over her perfectly adequate, flesh-covering outfit. If she emerged in another of those flirty dresses that showcased her phenomenal body…

Doomed.

Again, her long legs featured in an X-rated fantasy—naked, draped over his shoulders, the heels of her shoes digging into his back… If he were to break his one-time rule to quench the insatiable fire, it would just be sex, until the flames dwindled.

With a resigned sigh, he directed her towards the

restroom at the rear of the plane. He couldn't argue with her logic, though. Where their intense, combustive attraction was concerned, they were all out of options.

'Jacob, good to see you, man.' His old friend Lucas slapped him on the back with a shoulder bump and slid his delighted smile over Ash's shoulder to take in Essie. Ash had been right to fear her change of outfit.

She'd emerged from the plane's bathroom wearing a wisp of black silk that hugged her breasts and hips like a second skin and completely bared her back. A pair of skyscraper heels completed the visual suffering. She'd even scooped her swathe of golden hair up into some sort of relaxed up-do so the gorgeous translucent skin of her neck, shoulders and back paraded for his greedy eyes.

She'd sat opposite him for the remainder of the flight engrossed in her ever-present phone while he'd indulged in his lurid imaginings.

Further conversation was off the table, not because he wasn't curious to know more about her past—which not only held her in its grip, but seemed to have guided her choice of career—but because he feared she'd turn the spotlight on him. Pick apart his freshly opened wound with her insightful, analytical psychologist's mind.

He'd tried to get some work done, but the words on his screen had blurred in and out of focus. His mind had reeled from her scent and every time she'd shifted in her seat and he'd caught a glimpse of another sliver of skin, he'd had to dig his short nails into the leather of the arm rests to stop himself from peeling her out of the dress that had become an implement of torture.

Lucas, already endowed with that effortless French charm, looked at Essie as if he possessed X-ray vision and could clearly see the delights the dress barely concealed. Well, fuck that. For as long as it took to extinguish this all-consuming need—one surely brought on by something in the English water—Ash would be the only one sampling anything Essie had to offer.

While he'd tied himself in knots, fucking around with trust and rules and control, the answer had been staring him in the face all this time. He was never more composed than when in the bedroom. She'd said she could separate sex from their professional relationship. Time to test the theory. A win-win situation.

Ash placed his hand in the small of her back, wincing when she turned a sharp glance his way, presumably with the shock. He didn't need to explain his actions—he was done fighting this forest fire of need—and she'd suggested he take the driving seat. Time to buckle up, Ms Newbold.

'Lucas, this is Essie Newbold, my manager. I've told her all about La Voute, so thanks for the tour.' Now he wished he'd simply brought her to the club anonymously, because all he wanted to do was get her away from Lucas and onto the packed dance floor so he could legitimately put his hands on her some more and draw her close enough to feel those nipples.

Lucas laughed, took Essie's hand and pressed it to his lips.

Smooth bastard.

He held out his arm and directed them to the bar. 'The best way to enjoy La Voute is to experience it.'

The barman had clearly been pre-warned, because, on seeing the boss, he brought over a tray of luminous shots that glowed in the neon lighting as if radioactive.

'The house speciality. Enjoy.' Lucas handed one to Essie and, without taking his eyes from her, swallowed the second. 'I've reserved you a VIP booth upstairs.' Lucas replaced his empty shot glass on the tray and nodded to the barman. 'Make yourselves at home, drink whatever you want and, if you have any questions, you know where to find me.' He shook Ash's hand, which rolled into a fist when he turned to Essie and kissed both of her cheeks.

Ash forced a smile, a move that almost cracked his jaw, the tension in his facial muscles was so pronounced. He downed the shot and jerked his chin at the barman to indicate another round, getting himself back under control. He never succumbed to such puerile emotions as jealousy. What was she doing to him? Perhaps the extreme self-denial had infected his common sense.

'This is fantastic.' Essie's eyes sparkled as she bobbed in time to the music. She'd stood on tiptoes to yell in his ear but she hadn't touched him.

Ash nodded, his eyes dancing over the unselfconscious sway of her body to the beat.

'You asked Josh to create a house cocktail. I liked that. What else do you want to do to The Yard?'

Her wary eyes warmed at his simple compliment. 'I love that graffiti art over there.' She pointed to a wall of exposed brick decorated with vibrant tagging. 'We could do that in the basement, get an artist in. Use neon paint so it glows in the UV light.'

He nodded and bent closer, although he'd heard her

just fine. His own lips were only millimetres from her ear so her delectable scent curled around him like an aphrodisiac cloud.

'He's right.' He flicked his head in the direction Lucas had disappeared. 'Clubs like this have the X-factor. We should immerse ourselves, while we're here.' He handed her the second shot and tossed back his own with a grin of challenge. 'Let's dance.'

She eyed him while she slowly pressed the rim of the shot glass to her plump bottom lip, holding it suspended there for what seemed like an age, taking his stare captive. At the last second, the tip of her pink tongue poked out and dipped into the blue opaque drink. And then she tossed it, slammed the glass bottom up on the bar and turned for the dance floor with a sassy sway of her hips.

He groaned, adding *seriously fucking sexy* to her growing list of attributes. Ash followed, walking with his hard-on torture. He took Essie's elbow to keep them together as they weaved through the crowds. The crush of bodies moving under the strobe lights hemmed them in on all sides, forcing them to dance in the bubble of close personal space that suited his intentions just fine.

Essie's eyes widened as he palmed her hips and tugged her close. So he'd made an abrupt about-face? Better to switch tactics and settle than go into negotiations with a weak case. And it seemed this captivating woman weakened his body, his mind and his resolve.

He kept his hands and his stare on her, sliding his grip from her swaying hips to her slim waist as they moved in unison to the thumping beat. Her hands reached for his forearms, fingertips just shy of gripping. She closed her eyes, tilted her head back and lost herself to the music, as completely and perfectly as she lost herself to her pleasure.

His hands snaked to the small of her back and he hauled her tight up against him, the small gasp she made and the excitement in the eyes she snapped open spurring him on. His erection pressed into her soft belly. She knew the effect she had on him, one he hadn't been able to conceal since day one.

She gripped his shoulders, her bottom lip trapped between her teeth as she swayed against him, all sensual movements and lust-drunk eyes. They danced for half a track, heated stares locked, bodies bumping and hands lingering like the most exquisite form of tactile torture.

Fuck this. Fuck the club. If he didn't get inside her soon, he'd need another cold shower. And he was done with pale imitation. He held the real thing here in his arms. If she'd been a property acquisition, he'd have already closed the deal.

Ash bent close, his lips caressing her delicate ear. The cascade of fine tremors down her neck slammed steel through his spine. But before he could utter one word of his argument, she turned her head so her lips grazed his.

Her stare lifted to his and then dipped back to his mouth.

His fingertips pressed into her waist. 'You suggested we work this out. We'll do it in my bed.'

She leaned back, eyebrows lifted.

'We will?'

He shrugged. 'Or yours, or the couch or wherever. As long as it involves me inside you.' He lifted a tendril of hair from her neck and wrapped it around his index finger.

'I thought you only did one night?'

He could no more explain his about-turn than he could walk away. It was an astounding turn of events for a man used to making verbal arguments and teasing out favourable deals for a living.

He gripped her bare shoulder, his fingers gliding over her shoulder blade.

'I'm making an exception. And there's something of an experience gap to rectify, so I'm told.' His thumb caressed the dip above her collarbone, setting off more tiny shivers.

She pursed her lips, as if giving the matter some serious thought. Fuck, if he'd had any issue with his ego he'd be snivelling at her pretty feet by now. But he hadn't become one of New York's top attorneys by misjudging the opposition's intentions. She wanted this as badly as he did. He hadn't changed his stance on relationships, but they could still have a good time.

'Tell me what I need to hear,' he whispered.

'Just sex.' She wavered, her lip trapped under her teeth for a moment.

He nodded, her confirmation music to his ears. 'I agree.' He pressed his thumb to her bottom lip, tugging it free from her bite. The only thought in his mind—how quickly he could replace her teeth with his—drowned out all else.

Essie stepped closer until the length of her body pressed to his, her nipples grazing his chest, the heat between her legs scorching his thigh.

He tilted her chin up, his eyes dancing with hers.

'I'm not the guy for you if it's a relationship you're after.' He couldn't reiterate that enough, especially considering her past and her profession. Now more than ever he wasn't relationship material.

She dipped her chin, capturing his thumb with her pouty lips and sucking on the pad. She tongued his digit and then released him with a pop.

'I'm not interested in a relationship. And if I were, you'd be the last man I'd consider.'

Ash bit back a groan and rubbed his erection into the soft mound of her belly.

'So we agree. You chalk up a few more…notches on your casual sex bedpost. We fuck this out of our systems. Then we walk away.'

She lifted onto her tiptoes and he bent lower to meet her halfway. Her lips feathered his neck as she whispered, 'We keep it fun—when the fun stops, we stop.'

She peeled back, challenge blazing in her mesmeric stare.

'I can do fun.' Only this time he'd take his time, savour every sexy inch of her, glut himself until he was spent and sated and his head straightened out.

A single nod. 'What about the tour of the club?'

'I've seen enough.' His fingers curled over her hips, the silky fabric of her dress bunching in his grip. The way his body coiled to the point of bursting, he could tear the damn dress in two.

He'd never brokered a more fulfilling merger and, as with the best deals, everyone would get what they wanted. He rolled his shoulders and followed her from the dance floor.

As if it had been painted in luminous orange paint across the ground, he was about to cross a line he'd long ago vowed out of bounds. But damn if he didn't want to throw on a pair of sneakers and sprint over, hell for leather.

CHAPTER SIX

ESSIE PAUSED AT the foot of the stairs leading to the VIP booths, dragging Ash to an abrupt halt. His brow dipped and he faced her, clasping both her hands between them.

'Second thoughts?' He cupped her cheek, pushing back wild wisps of hair from her hot face.

It's just sex. Fun.

She fought the wave of trembles that doused her from head to toe and shook her head, and then tilted it in the direction of the bouncer guarding the upper balcony.

'Lucas said we had a VIP booth.' She caught her lip between her teeth. Her breath stalled as she waited for Ash to get on the same page. Every inch of her craved him. Slickness coated her inner thighs, her core clenched in anticipation and her nipples chafed against her dress with every rapid breath she took. She'd never make it back to the hotel before flinging herself on him and demanding what he'd held out on for so long.

'I've never experienced sex in a public place... That could be...fun.' She tilted her head, her fluttering heart knocking against her ribs. They'd either consummate this new agreement in the back of the limo Ash had hired to drive them to and from the club tonight, or they'd do it here, in the privacy of the VIP area of this chic, sophisticated club. She held her breath. When had she become such a risk-taking exhibitionist? What was he doing to her, this sexy but closed-off man, who at first glance seemed to have it all?

Ash's eyes scorched her. 'You want me to fuck you here? Upstairs?'

She nibbled the inside of her cheek, her flush hopefully hidden by the alternating dim and flash of neon lights. He'd suggested she broaden her horizons, something that worked for her out-of-control libido. What better way to build on the success of her first one-night stand? Keep things playful and risqué. Embrace the heady sense of power she earned from their no-strings encounters. If she focussed on the sex, she wouldn't think about anything else. Her doubts, her past, her bad decisions.

She nodded, her belly twisting with delicious spasms.

Ash's stare bored into hers while he clearly mulled over her suggestion. This bold, uninhibited demand was so unlike her. But this was what he did to her, what he brought out in her. And what she hoped like hell he'd embrace. She'd been turned on all day, all week. It was his fault—time to atone.

Because right now she barely recognised the wanton woman he drew out. Hormones raged through her. She pressed her thighs together to ease the persistent thrum of her clit.

Ash scooped his arm around her shoulders, nodded briefly to the bouncer manning the foot of the

stairs and escorted a tingling-from-head-to-toe Essie
to the upper balcony.

Essie tottered alongside his determined strides,
grateful he, too, saw the merits and timeliness of her
risqué plan.

At the top of the stairs, he swooped on her, hauling
her up with an arm around her waist and his hot and
greedy mouth, demanding an uninhibited kiss. Essie
clung, losing herself to the thrusting power of his
tongue sliding over hers and his strong arms banded
around her back, connecting them from shoulder to
thigh. Her head spun. This was happening.

Ash released her. 'You sure about this?'

She nodded, too turned on for speech. And too en-
thralled for doubts.

He strode ahead, tugging her behind. Now they'd
established the ground rules, he was all action. Thank
goodness. She didn't want to have to resort to begging
and pawing at him. So tacky.

The balcony overlooked the writhing mass of bodies on the dance floor below. To the left was a row of
discreet curtained-off booths, each lined with low,
banquette-style sofas and featuring an LED illumi-
nated coffee table. Ash led the way to the last booth
in the row, the one closest to what Essie guessed was
a door leading to a fire escape.

Adrenaline slammed through her, shunting energy
to every part of her body until her pulse thrummed
right down to her fingertips. Her senses heightened,
her skin buzzing under the glide of fabric, the music
vibrating through the floor and into her bones and
her vision eclipsed by the virile, determined man in
front of her.

Ash tugged her by the hand and flicked the gossamer curtains closed behind them. If someone came close enough, they'd see through the filmy barrier. But the angle from the ground floor provided sufficient privacy to keep Essie invested in her reckless, spur-of-the-moment idea.

He kept hold of her hand, his body close, taut with energy.

'You're astounding, do you know that?' He scanned her features with heated eyes.

She shook her head, her throat hot. If he didn't touch her soon, or allow her to touch him, she'd disintegrate into a million pieces.

He flared his nostrils, sucking in a breath, and then said, 'Take your underwear off.' A husky command. He held up his hand, palm flat, waiting for her offering. If that was his lawyer voice…he probably sealed every deal he touched.

Essie's blood turned to melted wax. Ignoring the liquidity of her limbs, she tilted her head, eyebrows arched. Who knew she housed such a perverse streak? He couldn't get his way all the time, even when his demands benefited her.

'You're a long way from Kansas, counsellor.' But she obliged, because this daring tryst had been her idea. No time for coyness now, not when she was finally getting what she'd craved since the day after she'd met him, when she'd foolishly raised the stakes with her secret scribblings about *Illegally Hot*. Time to be all in, or get the hell out of Dodge.

She braced herself steady with one hand on Ash's forearm, while she shimmied her panties down her thighs and then stepped out of them, one foot at a time.

Holding his self-satisfied stare, she dropped her damp thong in the centre of his palm, with as seductive a smile as she could manage. Why deny the effect he had on her? That he'd agreed to this told her he was equally affected.

Whatever else they were, physically they worked.

Ash glanced at the lace and then grinned, tucking it inside the back pocket of his jeans. With one tug he brought their chests and thighs and mouths back together.

'You—' he cupped her face and slanted his mouth over hers, eyes open, bold stare pinning her immobile '—have been driving me out of my mind for days.' He took her hand and pressed it to the steely length of him, guiding her to stroke him through his jeans, his hand over hers.

'I could say the same about you.' He was rock hard. She squeezed her thighs together, seeking a modicum of relief.

'With the exception of this rather unorthodox and public time, we'll be taking this slow. I intend to get my fill of you. To taste every part of you, over and over until neither of us can walk.'

'Another new experience. I can't wait.' Essie clung to him, her eyes just shy of rolling back. 'I thought you'd never break.' She looped her arms around his neck and tugged his mouth down to hers once more as she pushed him backwards towards the low upholstered seats lining the booth.

Through kisses, she fumbled with the button fly on his jeans until she'd freed his thick erection behind. He hissed, his hand covering hers to still her frantic fingers.

'This time, it's your rodeo.' He cupped her breast through the fine silk of her halter dress, his thumb stroking the nipple to a hard peak. 'Next time, and the multiple times after that, will be my way. Understood?'

She nodded, ready to promise anything to get what she wanted—him, inside her, losing his phenomenal control.

Ash fished a condom from his pocket with a wry twist of his mouth.

'I was a Boy Scout.' He handed the foil square to Essie and sat back on the banquette, his arms stretched along the back and his stare flitting between her bare legs, her pebbled nipples and her face.

Essie's mouth filled with saliva. He was hers to play with. Sprawled out beneath her, hard, ready and willing.

Forcing herself to sidle slowly with a seductive sway of her hips, rather than bound onto his lap with embarrassing eagerness as was her natural inclination, she sauntered close until her thighs slotted between his, which were spread wide, the prod of his manhood rising above his open fly.

Essie placed the condom on the seat next to him and lifted her dress above her knees. When his gaze left hers to follow the path of the hem, she slowed the progress down, enjoying the way air gusted from his nose with every rise and fall of his broad, sculpted chest.

As payback for torturing her with his impressive stamina, she stopped just short of showing him everything, instinct telling her Ash was a man who always got what he wanted in the end. She might as well draw out the anticipation. Keep him on his toes. Drip-feed him, until he snapped and took what he wanted.

With her thighs bracketing his, she straddled his lap, rising up on her knees to force his head back on the cushion so she could kiss him the way she'd longed to since this morning.

She traced his lips with hers and then repeated her path with the tip of her tongue. She cupped his face and angled his head so she could deepen the kiss—a tangle and slide of tongues that left them both panting for air.

He groaned and his arms left the back of the sofa, one banding around her waist to hold her close and the other sliding up her thigh until his fingers delved between her spread legs.

He hissed. 'Fuck, you're soaking.' His fingers probed her entrance from behind while his mouth settled hot and demanding over one taut nipple.

'Yes. It's your fault.' A whimper caught in her throat as he sucked hard through the silky fabric and then scraped with his teeth.

She released her hold on his hair to untie the straps of her dress, which were knotted behind her neck. She wanted him skin to skin. To feel his sexy day-old stubble scrape her nerve endings alive.

He obliged. With an impatient tug, he followed her lead and pulled the top of her dress down until both her aching, heavy breasts spilled free.

He cupped one, his hot stare tracing her while his thumb tortured the nipple again and again with rough swipes. 'So pretty.' Then he swooped, his mouth covering the glowing bud with long sucks and flutters from his talented tongue.

Essie dropped her head back, too strung out to hold in the moan of delight his fingers inside her and his mouth laving her breast unleashed.

He pulled back. 'You're going to have to stay quiet. We don't want visitors.'

Stay quiet? Was he aware how good he made her feel? She didn't give a damn if the whole of Paris rocked up with popcorn and opera glasses. But she didn't want him to stop, so she bit down on her bottom lip and focussed on the silvery wallpaper behind his head to battle the strong sensations he was thrusting upon her willing, eager body.

Essie cradled his head as he leaned in for another taste, but this time fiery jolts of electricity slashed from her nipple to her core.

Enough.

She tugged at the hem of his T-shirt and collapsed forward so her face was buried in his divine-smelling neck. After two or three impatient tugs on his shirt hem, Ash released her flesh and between them they removed his shirt with hurried jerks.

Ash tossed it aside while Essie just stared at him up close.

Despite the time he spent behind a desk or in a boardroom, he somehow maintained the ripped physique now laid out for her. She spread her fingers wide as her hands glided over the smooth tanned skin of his torso and tangled in the thatch of dark hair covering his pecs.

His fingers clutched the fabric at her hips, releasing and then gripping again while she took her time exploring him. She kissed a path down his neck, the stubble scraping at her sensitive lips.

A strip of black hair ran from below his navel and disappeared into his boxers, which were tented with his ready erection. As if she had been jump-started, she flew into action. She grabbed the condom and tore into it. Ash, equally eager, shimmied his jeans and boxers lower down his hips, releasing his cock, which bobbed on his hard, grooved belly.

Essie licked her lips. She wanted to taste every inch of him. But the clock was ticking. And if she didn't get him inside her soon, she'd burst from sexual frustration.

He grinned. 'Later.' His voice was so low, he sounded like a stranger. In many ways, all the important ways, he was. But just like the first time, she wanted him anyway.

'Don't worry.' He grinned. 'I want to eat you, too.'

She'd been right about the oral skills—she couldn't wait. She rolled the condom over the hard length of him, her movements hindered by the inferno burning her up from inside and his constant fondling of her breasts and rolling of her nipples between his fingers and thumbs.

And then she rose up over him, gripping him between her legs and angling him back towards her entrance. Ash shuffled his hips under her and she braced one hand on his shoulder while between them they guided him inside.

She sank, stretched and filled to perfection so a cry escaped. Ash covered her mouth with one hand, a reminder of their public location. Although the expression on his face—his bunched jaw, his flared nostrils, his hooded eyes—told her he, too, struggled to contain the intense bite of pleasure.

This was what she'd craved since she'd walked into

his office that fateful morning. His surrender to this flammable chemistry that rendered her helpless. She wasn't alone—confirmation was etched into the harsh planes of his taut features.

With his hand still clamped over her mouth, Essie began to move, rocking back and forth on his lap. The angle rubbed her in the perfect spot and she picked up the pace, bouncing on his lap with renewed energy, delivering what they both craved.

Ash settled back and gripped her hips, allowing her to dictate the angle and depth of penetration. But he didn't lay idle for long. One hand cupped her breast, tweaking and pulling her nipple until lightning snaked across her belly. The other hand delved between their bodies until the pad of his thumb settled over her neglected clit, strumming and circling.

'Yes,' she half hissed, half whispered. No way could she stay completely silent, not when he lay sprawled beneath her looking sexier than any sight she'd ever seen. And not when he filled and stroked her with sublime perfection.

When he started thrusting up from below, each blow accompanied by a harsh grunt while his big hands held her hips firm to hit the same spot over and over again, she lost all strength in her upper body and collapsed forward. Her hands clasped his sweat-slicked chest and her hair formed partial curtains before her face.

'Damn, you're tight. You clutch me just right.'

She whimpered, his verbal encouragement, his deep thrusts and his thumb back on her clit working a unique brand of magic over her body.

She gasped, flinging her wild hair back over her shoulders, her neck arched.

'That's it, ride me.' He panted out, his gruff commands low but no less insistent. 'I'm going to make you come so hard.'

With one last swipe of her clit and three rapid-fire thrusts of his hips, she climaxed, her whole body tense as she fluttered and clenched around him. Her cries bounced off the walls, but they were both past caring.

He sat up, buried his face between her breasts and clutched her to him with breaking force as he convulsed and groaned out his own climax.

Essie swallowed past her dry throat, gripping his shoulders while the spasms petered out and her heart slowed.

The sheen of cooling sweat stuck their clammy chests together. Essie caught her breath at last. 'Well, that was fun.' She buried her nose in his hair, stifling a giggle.

He kissed her breastbone, between her breasts.

'Hell, yeah, it was.'

She cracked up, taking him along with her.

CHAPTER SEVEN

ASH WOKE TO the melodic sound of distant church bells.

He opened his eyes to find the hotel suite, which was situated in Paris's Eighth *arrondissement*, bathed in filtered sunlight and his body wrapped around a soft, warm, sleeping Essie. His morning wood nestled between the cheeks of her spectacular ass. He ground his hips, the bite of pleasure damping down the flare of panic that waking up spooning a woman had created.

He never spooned. He rarely spent the night with someone, usually leaving after the business end of the evening was over.

He held himself rigid until the wave passed, its grip on his chest lessening until he could once again breathe.

They'd agreed.

Just sex.

Fun sex.

Astounding sex.

And, seemingly to test him to the hilt, she wanted to experience new and adventurous sex. Would he even survive? She'd been incandescent last night. First agreeing to his renegotiated terms of engagement and then stating her own, which aligned with his so beautifully that he had discovered breaking his cardinal rule was easy. For the right woman. The right…inducement.

And then she'd blown him away by suggesting they fuck in the very upmarket club that they'd come to vet. Who knew studious, bubbly, relationship expert Essie concealed such a libidinous inner vixen?

Lucky him.

He'd gladly expose her to previously untried experiences—a tough job that he relished. This was the perfect solution. Keeping things fun and playful clearly delineated the boundaries, gave him back the control he needed like oxygen. And provided an out clause—because this would end. Sooner or later the fun would dry up. And they could walk away. No feelings hurt. A good time had by all.

He breathed deeply, preparing himself, just as he did in negotiations—take control, brainstorm all possible outcomes and, if all else fails, railroad the opposition. With that strategy in mind, Ash shelved the niggling seed of doubt and gingerly untangled his limbs from hers without waking her.

By the time they'd returned to the hotel in the early hours of this morning, they'd been beat. They'd shared a quick shower and collapsed into bed.

And now he wanted his breakfast.

Sinking beneath the sheet with slow stealth, he manoeuvred himself between her thighs. Essie slept like the dead, so she didn't wake until he'd opened her up and wedged his shoulders between her shapely legs.

She stirred, her head lifting from the pillow to level sleepy eyes on him. Eyes full of dawning realisation.

Fresh lust pounded through him, his dick burrowing into the mattress. 'Morning. Ever experienced wake-up oral?'

She shook her head, bleary eyes rounded.

'Do you mind?' His voice was gruff, from the sight of her rumpled and vulnerable, her hair a wild tangle around her face, and from the vision of her open and glistening before him.

Her eyes were tinged with growing excitement. She shook her head but continued to stare. Waiting.

Ash touched the tip of his tongue to his top lip, catching the flare of heat in her eyes and the way her breasts rose and fell with her shallow pants. Her scent enveloped him. He shifted her thighs until she was splayed to his satisfaction.

Perfect, pink and pouty. The strip of fiery hair neatly trimmed framed the most exquisite sight he'd ever seen. One certainly worth waiting for. Who needed the works of art housed at the Louvre, when they had a naked Essie in their bed?

'Are you going to watch?' A surge of blood flooded his groin and she dropped her head back onto the pillow with a hoarse groan.

'I don't think I'll be able to.'

He tutted. 'Your choice. But I will. I recommend the experience.'

She looked at him again, her cheeks flushed pink. 'I…I've never come this way before.'

Heat bloomed in his belly. Man, he loved a challenge. 'You will for me.' Leaning forward, he opened her lips with his thumbs and touched the tip of his tongue to her clit. She jerked. Her thighs slammed against his head and her hands flew to his hair to hold him in place. Not that he was leaving. Not until he'd gorged himself and left her begging him to stop. Until he'd ruined her and set the bar sky-high.

He'd warned her last night and he never made idle threats. They weren't leaving this hotel room until neither of them could walk.

Sucking the tiny bud between his lips, he flattened his tongue and laved at her, over and over. He watched her every reaction: the way she fisted his hair in her hands; the way, despite her proclamation, she lifted her head from the pillows every few seconds to stare at the action occurring between her thighs; and the way she urged him closer by lifting her legs over his shoulders and digging her heels into his back, demanding more.

She swelled in his mouth, her breaths now coming hard and fast.

'Yes…oh…yes. You're so good at that—' Her breath caught on a keen wail. He winced as she twisted his hair, drawing back for a second to part her and slide two fingers inside her tight, velvety heat.

'Having fun?' He scraped his teeth along one inner thigh, delighting in the trembles that snaked across her flat belly.

'Yes. Yes. Don't stop.'

'I have no intention of stopping. Best breakfast ever.' He dived back in, this time matching the rhythmic laves of his tongue over her swollen clit to the plunging of his fingers, which he angled forward to rub her walls.

When she released his head so he could pluck and roll her rosy nipples, her neck strained as she held her head up to watch his every move and he knew she was close. He gave her everything, sucking and humming and plunging until she cried out, her voice a broken, thready cry that spoke directly to his pulsing dick.

He drew out the torture while she continued to clench around his fingers and then she pushed him away and collapsed back on the mattress.

'Oh, wow.' She laughed. 'That was definitely fun.'

He clambered up the bed to lie beside her. 'Glad I could oblige.' He pushed the wisps of hair back from her flushed face. 'Your exes were no good at that?' Responsive, sensual Essie had been cheated.

She turned to face him, propped on one elbow. 'Ex. Singular. He didn't like it.' Her cheeks darkened and Ash wished he'd kept his mouth shut.

What a douche. Some men didn't know what they had in front of them. Her finger snaked through his chest hair in slow, pensive circles.

'Of course, he didn't like the way I dressed or laughed or the friends I kept, either.' Her brittle laugh failed to lighten the mood.

So on top of her shitty father figure, her only boyfriend had been a controlling, insecure bully? Ash swallowed, half tempted to further ruin their morning by demanding the asshole's address and investigating how well he liked Ash's fist in his face. 'Did he...lay a hand on you.'

She shook her head and looked away, her colour now a blaze across her cheeks.

'There are other ways, verbal and emotional, to diminish someone. I put up with it for longer than I'm proud of.'

His chest turned to a block of concrete. 'It's okay.' He trapped her hand under his, stilling her fingers.

'Sometimes it's hard to see what's right under our noses.' Insightful, analytical Essie, so in tune with others' needs, would hate that she'd tolerated a bad relationship for herself, just as he hated his own blindness and misguided trust.

'Fun fact,' he said, grinning when she levelled sceptical narrowed eyes on him. 'That guy wasn't worthy of the tip of this finger.' He lifted her pinkie to his mouth and pressed a kiss to the tip. 'Let alone the rest of you.'

Couldn't she see that? Didn't she understand any man would be fucking lucky to have her? He would have…once.

Essie broke the dark direction of his thoughts with an energetic kiss, tugging on his neck and then climbing on top of him and sitting astride his thighs. She sat back and looked down at him, her beautiful face soft with desire and doubt.

He gripped her waist, questions banked up in his tight throat.

'We have to go back to London today.' Her words gave him pause as if she'd added, 'Back to reality.'

And Ben would return from New York. Would that alter their new arrangement? 'I know. Still time for a few more experiences though…' He could feed the desire and banish the doubt. Just fun.

She smiled, her hand encircling him and pumping with lazy strokes and the perfect amount of pressure.

'Have you ever been to Paris before?' he asked. The urge to offer more than new sexual experiences lifted the hairs on his arms. He wished they could stay a week. Wished he could wow her, wine her and dine her, as she deserved. Wished he could show her everything the French capital had to offer by day and indulge in her by night. All in the name of fun, of course.

Her thumb grazed the sensitive spot beneath his crown. He cupped her pert breast, his thumb tracing the dark tip. She shook her head, her mouth parting on a gasp and his balls rose up.

'We don't have enough time to see everything, but I've planned some sightseeing, if you'd like a whistle-stop tour.' Anything to put that sparkle back in her eyes.

She glanced at the window and the view beyond. 'Well, I can see the Eiffel Tower from here.' Her thumb traced the head of his cock, spreading the bead of moisture her stroking had released. Then her eyes lit up. 'Can we get real croissants?' She bit her lip, which he'd come to learn was her vulnerability tell, and a damned sexy sight.

He nodded, warmth from his gut spreading to his chest at her simple request. No Learjets or Tiffany baubles for this woman.

'Great.' She stopped rubbing him and jumped from the bed.

He recoiled, every muscle in his body taut and pulsing with energy to drag her back and bury himself between those thighs.

'Time for a shower, then, because I'm starving.' Instead of heading to the en-suite, she twisted her hair while her stare lingered on his still-raring-to-go groin. 'I've never experienced breakfast in the shower...'

Within seconds he'd hustled her into the bathroom and turned on the spray. She laughed and dragged him inside the glass cubicle, which was big enough for two.

Her mouth met his, her smile stretched wide. 'I

wanted to do this last night. I'm sorry I was so tired.' And then she dropped to her knees on the tiles and gripped the base of his straining cock.

His eyes wanted to roll closed, so good was the sight of her on her knees. But he forced them open. He spread his thighs as the water pounded his back and cascaded over his shoulders. Essie smiled a sultry smile up at him, pressed her tongue to the base of his shaft and licked a path to the engorged tip. He braced one hand on the glass, terrified his jerking legs would give out before the fun was over.

Her warm mouth engulfed him, stretching her pink lips around his head. He grunted, an animal sound he was certain he'd never made before, and then he cupped her face, tangling his fingers in her wild, wet hair. An anchor.

She sucked hard and swirled the tip of her tongue over the sensitive crown, lingering on the spot that left him growling out her name and clamping his jaw so tight he worried for his enamel.

The minx had the audacity to smile around him, her mouth full, and then she bobbed her head, her eyes locked with his, full of challenge while she moaned and mumbled. He surrendered. He was always going to lose this fight. The sight of her on her knees with his cock in her mouth one he'd remember for ever. She worked him higher until every muscle screamed.

She was fantastic. Why had he battled so hard to fight this attraction? His balls tightened and boiled and fire flickered at the base of his spine.

'Essie…' The warning clear, no doubt by the look of twisted agony on his face.

Humming encouragement against him, she nodded

her head, giving her permission. The flames licked along his shaft, lightning striking the tip at the moment he erupted on her tongue with a harsh yell and a slap of his hand on the tile.

She swallowed him down, releasing him with a pop and satisfied grin. He hauled her to her feet and crushed her close while she gripped his ass cheeks in both hands.

He pulled back, smacking kisses on her swollen, grinning lips.

'Best.'

Kiss.

'Fun.'

Kiss.

'Ever.'

Essie pointed her phone at the majestic gothic spires of Notre Dame and snapped some pictures. The private pleasure cruise Ash had booked took them down the Seine from the Eiffel Tower to the Pont de Sully and back. A perfect way to see so many of the city's iconic landmarks and to fully appreciate Paris's endless stunning architecture.

After they'd dressed, they'd spilled out of the hotel and found a charming Parisian café where they'd sat on the pavement at a gingham-covered table for two and feasted on warm crumbly croissants that melted in the mouth. This new experiences game they were playing left her floating on air. She'd even forgone posting on her blog for that day and switched off her phone in reverence to her first orally delivered orgasm and her first visit to the French capital.

Ash approached with two flutes of what was probably real champagne—she was too scared to ask, because today had already had enough of a fairy-tale quality to leave her both swooning and restless.

Because she'd woken up in Paris next to a gorgeous man, any woman's dream, who lived a lifestyle she couldn't comprehend—one perhaps, had her parents been married, had she and Ben grown up together, she might have glimpsed. But that wasn't her reality.

Her reality had been the role of odd kid out—not quite like many other kids from single-parent families but not quite like the whole families, either. Her reality had been years of loneliness, confusion and pining for an absent father. Yes, he'd sent endless gifts and she'd never gone hungry, but her reality had been an illusion. Just as her and Ash cruising the Seine drinking champagne was an illusion.

'You look sad—Paris not what you expected?' He sat next to her.

She shook her head. 'It's beautiful.' Her lip took a severe nibbling while she tried to marshal her conflicted thoughts. 'Your parents' divorce… Was it while you were growing up?'

Ash sniffed as if the warm summer air offended him. 'They're in the process of it right now, actually. Turns out my mother could tolerate one affair, but not two. Why?'

She took the glass of champagne he offered and sipped. 'Just imagining what your childhood was like.'

He looked away. 'Pretty normal, I guess.' He shrugged and slid his arm along the back of the seat.

'Did you come here with your family?' She picked

at the scab, imagining fun-packed but rowdy Jacob holidays. All five of them together.

He nodded, eyes wary.

Essie's glazed-over stare found the view again. 'I only remember one holiday with Mum and my father. I was ten.' The memories rushed in like a tidal wave, stealing the last of her high. 'I'd begged and begged to accompany him on one of his business trips to New York, promised I'd be so good he wouldn't know I was there. He appeased me with a trip to Chester Zoo.' She picked at a sliver of peeling paint from the seat. 'I didn't mind—it was the best trip ever. He bought me a stuffed elephant, we got our faces painted and he taught me to play chess back at the hotel.'

Ash's hand slid to her back, his palm warm between her shoulder blades, the rhythmic sweep of his thumb strangely unbearable.

'So you didn't see much of Frank?'

She shook her head, her face hot. Why had she even confided such a deeply personal moment with the power to shrivel her insides? The memory of what she'd done to that beloved stuffed elephant five years later when she'd finally discovered her father's deception still brought heat to her face.

'When I discovered the truth, that he'd lied to me and to Mum and his real family...' She met Ash's stare, shame and defiance warring inside. 'I...I built a bonfire in the back garden. It didn't end well for the elephant.'

Ash pulled her close and pressed his mouth to the top of her head, the gesture more than that of fuck buddy. But she wasn't naive enough to see Ash's display of romantic, even comforting, touches as anything but good manners and an attempt to keep their insatiable chemistry on the fun track where it belonged.

She sipped the frigid wine, pushing dark, dangerous thoughts away, and focussed on the view to stop the dangerous slide towards obsessing. It wasn't just the fact that Ash was way out of her league. He possessed a quick wit and was sexy personified. He had a dry sense of humour and regularly called her out on her more outrageous bullshit. A very addictive combination for a girl sadly lacking in healthy, long-lasting relationships, either in her own life, or displayed by her parental role models. A girl who'd spent two years in a dysfunctional, emotionally abusive relationship because she was so desperate to be the opposite of her parents.

She'd promised Ash she didn't want more than sex.

But if she ever changed her mind, ever considered herself capable of maintaining the kind of trust and commitment she frequently wrote about from a theoretical point of view, Ash represented exactly the kind of man she'd want.

Pity it was never going to happen. Not because he couldn't be sweet and romantic as he'd just proved, as well as an astounding lover. But because he'd meant what he'd said.

The ex Ben mentioned had clearly hurt him badly enough that he'd sworn off anything beyond casual for good. Those closest had the most power to cause lifelong pain.

She shuddered. She'd certainly never been back to a zoo.

'Oh, look.' She latched onto a distraction and pointed at a couple on the walkway lining the riverbanks. A bride and groom, having their picture taken.

Ash followed the direction she indicated, and they stared for several stilted, silent seconds. Essie squirmed, covering the awkward moment with a blast of verbal diarrhoea to put him at ease.

'Ah, the city of love... Oh, fun fact. Did you know that falling in love has the same effect on your brain as snorting cocaine?' She wasn't fishing for a proposal, but she wasn't carved from stone like the gargoyles atop Notre Dame. Just because love hadn't worked out for her parents, for her, perhaps for Ash, didn't mean others couldn't find it.

Ash looked away from the beaming couple, his stare skittering anywhere but on Essie.

'Did you know the divorce rate in the Western world averages fifty per cent?' He curled his lip and sipped his wine.

She gaped. She wasn't wholly surprised—if more men were like her father and her ex...and his father... His cynicism was more than a hardened lawyer thing—it must be the woman...

The set of Ash's mouth told her now wasn't the right time to pry. Time to drag the conversation back to fun town. 'I didn't. But you're ruining the ambience, counsellor.'

He shrugged, a smile on his face, but his shoulders didn't drop to pre-shrug levels.

She rolled her eyes. 'Don't worry. I'm not hinting.' She nudged him with her elbow, trying to lighten the mood. 'From a scientific standpoint, I find it fascinating that something as nebulous as—' she made air quotes '—"love" is powerful enough to induce such a rush of euphoria on a neurological level.'

He stared for long silent seconds.

Essie brazened it out, but inside she wanted to roll into a ball and protect her soft parts.

'Do you really believe all that relationship babble?'

She bristled. Had he just ridiculed the basis of her entire research doctorate? The foundation of her precious and increasingly popular blog? The very doctrine she hoped to live the rest of her happy and contented life by, next time she was brave enough to dip a toe back into relationship waters? At least next time she met someone, she'd also have a sexual standard to measure them against, thanks to Ash.

For the first time in her life, she knew what all the fuss was about.

'I don't need to believe it. Just because we've never experienced it—it's science.'

'It's bullshit.' He flushed and then winced. 'It may be science, but science isn't for everyone. It isn't for me.'

Essie's heart rate accelerated. He was opening up. Had her earlier confessional mood infected him?

'Without changing my plea, I meant what I said last night—just fun—why the hefty dose of cynicism?' She glugged more champagne in case this conversation blew up in her face. The psychologist in her couldn't help but pry. And the woman who'd had fantastic sex with him was pretty interested, too.

She couldn't look too closely at why, preferring to believe her interest was a side effect of the spectacular orgasms, professional curiosity or her constant need to help her fellow man.

With his eyes shielded behind sunglasses, she had no non-verbal cues to help—Ash sat as still as a statue.

'I had a fiancée. Years ago. I thought myself in love, the kind you think exists, scientifically.'

Essie's throat tightened until she expected to hear choking sounds when she breathed. She clamped her lips shut, desperate for him to continue. To learn more about this closed-off man who had so much to offer and what had shaped him.

'Right up to the week before the wedding, when I discovered she was cheating on me.'

Essie stared, mouth agape.

Who would cheat on Ash?

A splash of icy champagne spilled on her dress, soaking through the fabric. She looked down, busying herself with wiping at the spill with the hem of her dress, to both gather her own scattered thoughts and give Ash some time to recover from his shocking confession.

But what did she say to a temporary lover on discovering he had indeed had his heart broken, something that had tainted all his future relationships? She knew what psychologist Essie would say. She even had an idea how relationship blogger Essie would handle it. But the woman who'd spent the night in his bed and was already struggling with the boundaries she'd agreed to Essie? She was all over the place.

'Have you...had anyone serious since then?'

He shook his head, confirming her theories. 'Casual works best for me.'

While part of her was happy that she and Ash were on the same page in their personal reasons for avoiding relationships at this stage in their lives, his confirmation came with an unpleasant hollowness in her stomach.

He'd really meant what he'd said.

'I'm sorry you were hurt. Your ex sounds a couple of sandwiches short of a picnic, if you ask me.' Humour seemed the safest option to claw back the light-hearted, Parisian vibe they'd had earlier. But it didn't banish the gnawing inside, or the restlessness of earlier. Or the urge to comfort Ash. But he'd hate that. She sat on her free hand.

Ash shrugged. 'I'm well over it. As I said, it was years ago.' He didn't appear over it. In fact, a greenish hue tinged his skin. 'I just think that whatever that emotion is—that drug-like high—it passes pretty quickly, and then what do you have?'

She had plenty of answers, but none she thought he'd want to hear. And perhaps he was right. What did she really know? Everything she'd learned about men came from her ex, a pathetic excuse for a man who'd needed to put her down to make himself feel like a man, and her waste-of-space father—a man who was only in her life thirty per cent of the time and never at the important moments. If she'd grown up with Ben, at least she'd have had a stable male role model, an older brother to fight her corner, vet her boyfriends and tell her she was worthy. But Frank had robbed her of that, too.

'Love didn't work out for you and the lazy, critical, controlling jerk-off...' He toyed with a strand of her hair, his stare searching.

'No.' As far as romantic relationships went, she'd proved her judgment was seriously lacking. She'd accepted meagre scraps, just like her mother. 'But that was my fault. People treat you the way you allow yourself to be treated, right?' Yes, she knew the theory down to the last detail, but putting it into practice for yourself... That was another matter.

Ash nodded in agreement, his stare fixed on the horizon.

'But, you're right. I haven't found it, yet. But I do know that as humans we're destined to strive for a meaningful connection, an interaction with other humans. We can't avoid it. It's evolutionary. A survival tactic.'

'Is that why your relationship with Ben is so important?'

Essie shrugged, feigning indifference while her insides shrivelled. 'You don't have to be a psychologist to see I have daddy issues. I grew up thinking I was an only child. I loved my father, idolised him as a little girl, but his betrayal ruined our relationship.' She shrugged, playing down the impact of her rolling stomach. 'I feel cheated—Ben's a great guy, as you know.'

Ash nodded.

And Ash? Another great guy who'd been hurt in the past, who she'd objectified on her blog in order to feel validated. Well, that ended today. No more *Illegally Hot*. And no more crazy ideas about Ash being anything more than a temporary fling.

Several beats passed.

'Hungry?' said Ash.

Essie nodded, despite her swirling stomach.

'Let's go to Montmartre for lunch. They have a street market today.'

And just like that they successfully hurdled the invisible barrier—with good, old-fashioned denial.

CHAPTER EIGHT

THE FOLLOWING SATURDAY night Ash emerged from The Yard's offices to find the bar awash with smart, glamorous opening-night customers. Cocktails and good times flowed. Essie and Josh had organised a happy hour to bring in office workers, and the online social media buzz she'd created had ensured it was standing room only. Their brand-new cocktail menu was inscribed in elegant script on the oversized contemporary chalkboard behind the bar. Every glass sparkled. The bar's state-of-the-art lighting created pockets of ambience, certain nooks and crannies of the chic space becoming intimate, dimly lit corners.

But instead of the satisfaction he'd anticipated, his body was strung taut, every muscle twitchy. Ash scanned the bar for Essie. He knew she wore the same slinky black dress she'd had on at La Voute a week ago, because just before they'd opened The Yard's door for the first time, she'd strode into his office with that slightly feral gleam in her eyes, locked the door behind her and perched her delectable derrière on his desk.

When she'd slowly bared her thighs, revealing that she'd removed her underwear, he'd been powerless to resist what had followed—him fucking her on his desk, a new experience she'd requested with a cheeky, 'For luck…?'

The restlessness dissipated as he recalled the past week of fantastic sex. They'd spent practically every spare minute screwing—starting with the flight back from Paris to London, where she'd ridden him in one of the wide leather seats at thirty-thousand feet, successfully earning herself a mile-high experience, and continuing at work, at his apartment and anywhere else they could get away with. The intense, couldn't-keep-their-hands-off-each-other phase was lasting well beyond the arbitrary time limit he'd set. Any day now, he expected the bubble to burst, the novelty to wear off, the fun to end and his life to return to normality.

But the desire was far from abating and Ash found himself in new territory.

Perhaps the out-of-body feelings rattling him were a symptom of having allowed the insatiable, enthusiastic Essie too much time in the driving seat? Time to wrestle back some of the control, dictate the…fun, suggest the next experience. His mind whirred with endless pornographic possibilities. Yes, that was just the right tactic to steer things back on track.

He spotted her at the far end of the bar and discreetly adjusted himself. She still carried the radiant glow her earlier orgasm had delivered to her translucent skin. She'd retamed her hair, twisting it into some messy topknot that left only a few wisps tickling her elegant neck. Just knowing that the halter dress she wore prevented her wearing a bra, and that her perfect tits were bare under the scrap of silk, flooded his groin with fresh heat. Heat that should have dissipated after their quick but thoroughly satisfying desk session. But no. It was as if the more he had, the more he knew about her, the more he wanted.

A very dangerous combination.

Ash set off towards the object of his disgruntlement, weaving his way through the throng. She chatted with Josh, who smiled at her and touched her arm. Essie laughed at something he said as she leaned close to speak over the general din of a hundred conversations and the vibratingly loud music.

Ash pressed his lips together and swallowed down the taste of acid. 'Fucking fantastic…'

A thump to his shoulder pitched him off balance.

'Go easy on her, man,' said Ben, who'd sneaked up behind him. Ben grinned at his friend and then looked at Essie, an indulgent smile playing on his mouth.

Ash slapped Ben's shoulder in greeting, his own shoulders cramping with the tension of lusting after Ben's sister. Add to that the very foreign stabbing pain under his ribs as he watched Josh and Essie together… He needed a lie-down and it was only eight thirty.

'She can't help helping people—it's who she is.' Ben stared at the couple chatting as if he was as enamoured as Ash, although likely in a different way.

He nodded as he flicked his gaze back to where she conversed with Josh. He could just imagine the kind of help the hipster barman wanted.

He'd developed quite an insight into Essie's magnificent, multifaceted personality. She was so different— different from him, a cynical, cut-throat lawyer with a reputation of being just like his ruthless old man; from most people he knew—out for themselves, inward-looking, selfish; and from any other woman of his experience, which was probably why he struggled to put a stop to their sex spree.

She was too good for him. Too good for her spineless ex and her careless father, too.

She laughed with Josh, her head tilting towards him in that way that made a person feel she was truly listening.

Fuck. He would hurt her when this ended. Yes, she'd said what he'd wanted to hear, but his instincts about her had been correct—Essie was a relationship kind of girl. She'd just lost her confidence at the hands of the worthless men in her life.

Ben loosened his tie. 'Josh is having boyfriend trouble,' he said. 'Essie can't resist a distress signal.'

Ash grinned, his head now so light it practically lifted off his shoulders.

Josh was gay.

As soon as he'd registered the relief pouring through him, it morphed into something else, something not unlike the itch of head-to-toe poison oak. What place did jealousy have in his orderly, controlled life? What place did any feelings have where Essie was concerned? She wasn't his—because that was the way he wanted it. Insisted on it. Made crystal clear from the outset. Why, then, did his insistence sound entirely self-directed?

'Hey, can you grab her? I have something I want to say to both of you.' Ben tilted his head to indicate the cordoned-off stairs leading to the basement dance club, which was quiet for now, but would soon be heaving with partygoers, if their ticket sales were any indication.

'Sure.'

Ash resumed his way across the bar to Essie, the idea of ending things tonight forming in his mind. Halfway there, she spotted him and he rebelled against the idea with a violent mind spew.

Whatever she'd been saying to Josh stalled on her lips, which hung a little open as she levelled her wide stare on an approaching Ash. Fire licked his balls. He'd come inside her not two hours ago. And already he wanted her again. She could do that to him with her open smile or her ready, but dirty, laugh. Even her irritating fun facts lent her an irresistible and refreshing air you couldn't help but adore.

He skirted around her and bent low from behind to speak in her ear—it was a club after all, the noise levels rendering that perfectly acceptable.

'Ben wants to see us downstairs.' A satisfying trill of shivers passed down her neck. Oh, yes, she battled the same hunger raging in him. Thank fuck he wasn't alone. Because that hunger was the only thing keeping him on an even keel.

Just sex—his rule.

Just fun—her rule.

He swallowed the panic and pressed his mouth to her ear. 'And I want to see you naked and splayed open for me,' he whispered. That would give her something to ruin those lacy thongs she wore, probably for his torment.

She tilted her hips and pressed her ass up against his groin, at the same time as leaning forward across the bar to tell Josh she'd talk to him later.

Not if he had anything to do with it—she'd be too busy coming around the cock she'd just flicked back to life with her sassy stunt. She knew exactly what she was doing, but payback would be fun.

He put his hand in the small of her back where the dress dipped low and led her downstairs. Her skin burned his palm. Her feminine scent buffeted his senses. And if he slid his hand a couple of inches south he could cup those rounded ass cheeks and ascertain if she'd donned the panties again after the desk session...

At the last minute, he inwardly bit out a curse and dropped his hand from her skin, seconds before they entered the VIP booth where Ben waited.

He'd opened the good stuff—Cristal. Three tall contemporary flutes sat on the table next to a small gift-wrapped package. Ash bit the inside of his cheek. He'd thought about giving Essie an opening-night gift, but he'd talked himself out of it, too terrified by the impulse and too worried it would blur the rigid lines he'd demarcated.

Ben kissed his sister's cheek and poured the bubbles with a flourish. Ash struggled to share his friend's enthusiasm. When they were all seated with a glass in hand, Ben raised his for a toast.

'I just wanted to thank you both for all your hard work these last two weeks, and for holding the fort while I was away. We wouldn't be here, opening night, without you two...so cheers. To The Yard.'

Ash and Essie joined the salutation, their eyes meeting briefly. Ash saw in her expression what he guessed was mirrored in his own—a flash of guilt. Fuck.

What with the new and dangerous emotions ensnaring him, and considering the potential mess when this ended for him, for Essie, for his friendship with Ben…he should be a man. End it tonight, on a high.

We opened the club…what say you we call this quits and part as friends?

The mouthful of wine soured. He made a fist under the table.

'And, Essie…' Ben collected the gift and handed it to her '…I want you to have this. Thanks for stepping in when I needed you.' Ben stared, earnest, while Essie looked at him as if he'd just saved her, single-handed, from a burning building. And fuck if Ash didn't want to see her level that look in his direction, equilibrium be damned.

'As a kid, I always wanted a sibling.' Ben swallowed, visibly moved. 'I'm just glad it's you.'

She took the package, her lower lip trembling. As she fumbled with the bow and the paper, an unseen force made Ash reach discreetly beneath the table to touch her knee in silent support. This developing bond with her brother fed her soul, healing the cracks her father had created with his callous selfishness. Her old man and that douche of an ex had really done a number on her self-esteem. But Ash had underestimated the depth of her longing to be a part of Ben's life. To have more of a family. To belong. She deserved those things.

Ash had grown up surrounded by his family. Until recently he'd worked alongside them, every day. His sisters were still, and always would be, a massive part of his life. What must it have been like to never know when your parent was going to drop by? To wonder if this time, this birthday would be different? To feel unworthy of their time and attention, something that was a fundamental part of the parental role in Ash's opinion. He knew all about shitty fathers... But at least he'd grown up knowing he'd mattered to both parents.

He gripped her knee tighter. The next time he saw Frank Newbold...

Essie flashed him a brief, grateful smile and then she tore through the last of the paper and looked on in wonder. Ash forced his fingers to relax. She wasn't his business. They were just having fun.

It was a framed snap of Essie and Ben outside The Yard, their arms around each other and their grins, so alike, wide and beaming.

Essie's eyes filled and she threw her arms around her brother's neck.

Ash stilled, his breath trapped, a voyeur, an outsider on the growing sibling connection between these two. But he couldn't look away, or leave. A sick part of him forced himself to see what his selfish, indulgent actions put at risk. The siblings stood for a proper hug. Essie turned her face, which was pressed to Ben's chest.

Part of him had genuinely believed their chemistry would have petered out by now. That the insistent itch would have dissipated. But if anything, the need only intensified. Because now he knew Essie. He understood her quirky sense of humour. He could laugh at her strange English phrases and the way she'd translate them for his transatlantic education, and he reciprocated her enthusiastic desire for him, which seemed equally insatiable and only built in intensity with every day that passed.

Despite knowing the cost of deceit and betrayal—especially from a family member, one you should be able to trust with your life—the damage they wreaked. Despite knowing her past left her craving this relationship with Ben. Despite breaking his rules to have her only once, his resolve was steadfast. He couldn't, wouldn't offer her more than what they had right now. But was he ready to give her up?

He couldn't be what she needed. He owed it to her, to his friend, to let her go now, before the toll of his selfishness grew.

His blood stilled as if turned to concrete. Before he could make an excuse and leave on some pretext or other, he heard familiar voices. He turned around in time to see his sister, Harley, and the others arrive. *Perfect timing.* He'd forgotten they were coming to The Yard's opening night, he'd been so busy losing himself in Essie.

Harley flew at him with a squeal of excitement. He lifted her into a bear hug. She'd arrived from the States today with her fiancé, Jack, who split his time between Europe and New York.

Ash gripped his sister tighter than usual, earning him a searching stare when he released her to the ground. At least his sister hadn't blamed him for his part in their parents' split. She, too, had had her fingers burnt with Hal.

'You look amazing.' He kissed her cheeks, forcing his fingers to relax on her shoulders, and then shook hands with Jack and, behind them, Jack's friend Alex and his fiancée, Libby. Ash made introductions and the group settled around the table as a waiter brought more glasses and a second bottle of Cristal.

Essie, Libby and Harley quickly fell into animated and excitable conversation and the other men started a debate about some upcoming English soccer game Ash had no clue about. He sipped his drink, a sense of unease capturing him as he watched the interactions around the table, as if from a distance. He'd done enough emotional wrangling for one night. Damn, enough for a whole year. But the unwanted thoughts pushed their way into his head anyway.

Fraud.

Outsider.

Pretender.

He almost snorted champagne out of his nose. He'd long ago sworn off wanting what his sister and Jack's friend had. So why now did the hair at the back of his neck react to every look the couples shared, every touch, every unspoken communication? Because he knew he was short-changing Essie, like the men of her past.

He focussed on Essie, whose cheeks had pinked up nicely with the alcohol. She participated fully in the conversation with the other two women, who, Ash understood, had become close friends in recent months. But her gaze slid often to him, secret, non-verbal cues passing between them with every flick of her expressive eyes.

She was happy.

Ash's unease lessened. Perhaps he was overthinking this. She'd never hinted she wanted more than sex. Great, addictive sex. He should go with the flow tonight. Enjoy his and Ben's and Essie's success. Enjoy his sister's company and that of new friends.

The next time she looked up, he smiled back at Essie, his spirit lightening. During a brief lull in the chatter, Harley cleared her throat.

'So, we have something to ask you.' She glanced around the group, her eyes finishing on Jack.

Ash's shoulders tensed to the point of cramping as chills raced down his spine. Harley looked far too happy.

'We're getting married. Monday,' she said with a flourish and giggle.

The blow winded him. Married? They'd only just reconnected.

'What? Since when?' Ash reeled, his stomach tight.

Harley nodded, barely containing her joy. 'It's all arranged—we just planned it in the car on the way here.' She leaned over to kiss Jack while the others offered congratulations and indulgent grins.

Of course. Because that was how most people planned the most important commitment of their lives—spur of the moment. He hated to be the voice of doom, but they'd only been engaged a few months... And they had history.

More importantly, had she learned nothing from his experience? From their father's appalling behaviour, towards their mother, Harley herself and most recently towards Ash? All done in the name of so-called love.

Yes, he'd jumped in too soon, his engagement to Maggie impulsive, flushed with the enthusiasm of first love. And look where that had led. To heartbreak, and humiliation. To the ultimate betrayal. Its effects long-lasting, shaping him, controlling him, affecting his precious equilibrium even to this day. Affecting his ability to be open to someone new in his life.

He'd thought himself over it years ago, but now, years later, its effects still carried power. Because the lies outlasted all else. Discovering Hal had been the real partner in Maggie's betrayal and that he had concealed it from Ash, from everyone, long after the affair ended, had sealed the fate on both his working relationship with his father and his personal one. Ash's whole life as he'd known it had, in an instant, become untenable. His stomach rolled. He couldn't bear to look at his father, let alone work with the man.

'What about New York? Mum and Hannah?' No way would Harley marry without her twin sister present. And was Hal flying in for the ceremony? He couldn't be in the same room as him. Not yet. The betrayal was still too raw.

And what about divorce and infidelity and lies? He hadn't exaggerated when he'd informed Essie of the reality of divorce statistics. And he'd seen enough professionally—inevitable prenups, prolonged bitter wrangling over assets, the financial and emotional toll of a commitment that seemed like a good idea at the time but didn't last. Not to mention his personal prejudices...

'Mum and Hannah are flying in tomorrow. We don't want a big fuss, just a simple service. Alex said we can have the ceremony at his estate in Oxfordshire— this is what we want.' She clutched Jack's hand, some freaky silent communication passing between them. 'We'll celebrate with extended families separately.'

Ash could understand. There was no way their father and Jack's parents could attend the same event, not after they'd recently discovered the reason for the long rift between the former friends was another historic affair between Hal and Jack's mother. What a selfish bastard his father had turned out to be. He'd always known he was arrogant and uncompromising, but he hadn't realised he was such a shitty human being. Once a cheater, always a cheater.

Surely these were all perfect reasons for Harley and Jack to employ caution. To get to know each other better. To allow their relationship to stand the test of time before marriage. Why the hell did they have to marry at all? Why not just live together?

It warmed him that Harley, who'd struggled growing up because of her dyslexia, was happy. But could he stand to watch her go through the devastation a wrong choice now would bring? Jack seemed crazy about her, but you never really knew what lurked inside someone. Everyone had their ugliness.

As Harley turned to Ben and Essie, including them in the invitation to Oxfordshire, Ash battled his helplessness. It seemed, unless he could talk her out of this, he'd have a ringside seat. The least he could do was offer her some legal advice for when the shit splattered through the blades of the fan.

CHAPTER NINE

ASH TOYED WITH the ends of her hair, which still clung to his damp chest and the day's worth of stubble on his chin. Even at three a.m., after two rounds of opening-night celebratory sex, the oblivion of sleep evaded him.

Essie's head grew heavy. Had she succumbed to exhaustion? Should he slide out from under her and pound out the continued restlessness in the gym?

'Just tell me, Ash.' Her sleepy voice whispered over his skin, a soft caress that offered both release and a rising of his hackles. His body stilled but she stayed immobile and he was pinned beneath her sprawled, languid body.

'The problem shared, problem halved thing is true, you know.' She lifted her head and levelled warm, compassionate eyes on him. 'I won't judge you. I won't even comment. I'll just listen.' She settled her head back on his chest, but not before she brushed her lips over his skin with a small sigh.

Seconds stretched while he balanced on the edge, wishing he could be as brave and open as she was.

He could deny he had anything to confess.

He could huff and puff his way out of it.

He could even feign sleep.

But he wouldn't insult her intelligence.

With a sigh that lifted and then dropped her head, he drew his fingers back through her hair. The silky slide of the strands carried a hypnotic cadence he craved. Or perhaps it was just Essie.

'I think she's rushing into marriage.'

Coward.

True to her word, Essie remained quiet. Only her heartbeat, steady but fast enough, beating against his, indicated she was still awake.

'I've made no secret how I feel about it.'

She nodded, the slide of her skin and hair over his chest a soothing kind of torture, because it drew him out, a security blanket, lulling him to deeper confessions, ones at his very centre.

'You're probably thinking I have a right to feel the way I do. I told you about my fiancée, my parents splitting recently, my insider knowledge of the divorce courts from law school.'

He was making a meal of this. Was it better to say the words outright, to rip off the bandage with a vicious tear, that would bleed him out quicker, but shorten the sting? Or keep them in and protect himself.

'I discovered my father had cheated. More than the affair my mother knew about.' Essie stopped breathing and her pulse thrummed against his skin. 'I was the one who had to deliver that news. I didn't want her to hear it from someone who didn't care about her.'

Her head lifted, tugging her hair from between his fingers, her face wreathed in understanding.

'That must have been horrible for you.' She sat

up, crossing her legs and drawing the duvet into her lap to cover her nakedness. 'How did *you* find out?'

Ash nodded, the urge to flee the room and the shameful scrutiny strong. If he'd detected one hint of pity in her expression he'd already have hit the shower, but Essie's brow pinched in confusion.

'From the horse's mouth—my father told me. We'd…had a disagreement. He didn't like the way I'd dared to call him out on his bullshit so he lashed out, like he derived pleasure from inflicting the knowledge on me. The coward knew I'd tell her.'

He linked his hands behind his head as he shrugged it off.

'Some people are cowards. I understand your fears for Harley.'

'I just worry that she'll be hurt. As it is, she's marrying without her father present and our mother…' He sucked in a breath, and rose to sit on the side of the bed. 'She didn't know about that particular affair until I informed her.'

He swallowed bile. 'It turned out to be the last straw for her.' He stood and made his way to the door of the en-suite. 'So, you understand my trepidation about this…happy occasion?'

Essie's teeth worried at her lip, her eyes scraping him raw.

Tell her. Tell her everything.

He backed away. She had the sense to give him space.

He stepped under the steamy blast of the shower, welcoming the pound of the water as a replacement for the waves of self-directed emotion. He was a coward, too. Holding back, convincing himself he was happy. That he was justified in his mistrust.

And he still carried the full burden of guilt and self-loathing, not the half measure Essie had promised.

She joined him, as he'd known she would. She'd kept her promise, but offered silent comfort, just by her presence. Her touch, tentative at first, as if she was uncertain of her reception, grew bolder. She reached for the body wash and tipped a measure into her palm before sliding soap-slicked palms over his chest, abdomen and shoulders. When she moved behind him to soap his back, she pressed her mouth between his shoulder blades.

'I'm sorry that happened to you. Do you want me to go home?'

He turned to face her, scooping his arm around her waist and hauling her up so his mouth covered hers. 'No.'

Within seconds their lazy kisses grew torrid. Her slippery skin slid against his as she writhed and moaned in his arms, her hands clutching at him. Her fingers twisted in his wet hair and she angled his head and twisted her mouth away. 'I want you.'

He'd recovered sufficiently to be fully on board. Slamming off the water, he scooped Essie up and lifted her from the shower. In two strides, he'd deposited her on the bed, still sopping wet, and fell to his knees between her spread thighs.

His mouth covered her, a hint of soap and whole lot of delicious Essie. He worked her higher, her moans and gasps telling him when the time was right. With a curse, he tore his mouth from her and quickly covered himself with a condom.

When he pushed inside her, she gripped his face, her blue stare burning into him in unspoken unity.

They climaxed together, eyes locked, cries mingling and the blurred and broken lines of fun scattered all around them.

Getting out of London, especially for the romance of an impromptu wedding at one of the UK's most lavish private estates, complete with a boutique winery and hotel, carried a surreal quality akin to flying to Paris, just to go clubbing. Essie, giggly with excitement, relaxed back into the leather upholstery of Ash's Mercedes, and tried not to drool at the confident, manly way he handled the luxury car.

It was the same confident, manly way he handled everything, especially when commanding her pleasure with skilled, devastating proficiency.

Ash was quiet, a fact she wanted to attribute to him driving on unfamiliar roads, but she couldn't deceive herself after his late-night revelations. What should have been a joyous family occasion had huge potential to become a trigger. Hers wasn't the only dysfunctional family in the world.

Essie shifted in the seat, restless.

That Ash had opened up to her on Saturday night enclosed her in a warm cocoon. She longed to reassure him about today. That his own pain at being left by his fiancée would pass. That his mother surely didn't blame him for stepping up. That his sister had her own life to live with a man who wasn't Hal Jacob.

Perhaps he regretted opening up to her. Many men struggled to talk about their feelings. She'd bide her time. He had enough going on with his family drama.

She'd spent all of Sunday, after a late start, where she'd crawled home from Ash's apartment to catch up on mundane life things like laundry and bill-paying and checking on her flatmate. Of course, she also had to catch up on her latest blog post, entitled *Love is in the air—is it catching?* It was wedding season, after all. She glanced over at Ash, prickles of guilt dousing her high.

Her blog continued to attract new followers and the ads she'd incorporated on her website, featuring well-respected books on relationships, had high click-through rates. People couldn't get enough of *Illegally Hot*, if the comments were any indication. But she hadn't mentioned him in the last few posts. His pain was real—not entertainment fodder.

In the beginning, writing about her overwhelming attraction to Ash and his extreme bedroom skills had helped control the impact he'd had on her life. Helped her to rationalise that she was simply, for the first time, party to a healthy, equal-terms relationship based on spectacular sex. But now... She shuddered. Every social media mention, every new follower, every demand for more of *Illegally Hot* carried with it a hundred tiny barbs to her conscience.

Perhaps she should confess. Explain why she'd done such a reckless and thoughtless thing.

No. She'd never actually used any identifiers— he'd never know he was *Illegally Hot*. He'd never read the blog. And this wouldn't last for ever—Ash would move on and she would chalk up this experience and believe in herself and what she had to say.

Because she was no longer Essie the downtrodden, the ignored, the inconvenient. She was part of something wonderful, respectful and mutually satisfying. And with a man as incredible as Ash.

And her relationship with Ben was also looking up. Essie hugged the memory of his thoughtful present to her chest. She'd all but sobbed over him on Saturday night.

I always wanted a sibling... I'm just glad it's you.

That he would make such a heartfelt declaration went a long way to healing the past hurts and humiliations inflicted by their father. Ben respected her. He was starting to value her as a part of his life, as her inclusion in today's nuptials proved.

Ash exited the A40 to Oxford and headed into the green and gold countryside. The sun glinted off fields of barley, filling Essie with a momentary sense of the contentment she'd craved her whole adult life. She was spending time with her brother and his friends, welcomed into his social circle.

An equal.

Valued.

Important.

'What do you think of our English countryside?' So Ash wouldn't want to talk about Saturday night, or the wedding today, but they could still converse.

'Very pretty.'

'Don't you miss New York?' Of course she understood why working with his father at the family firm would be awkward, but why set up shop in London, why move away from your entire life?

He shrugged, non-committal. 'The Jacobs are never absent from the business pages or the gossip columns for long.' He concentrated on the road, his mouth a grim line. But Essie was more concerned about the growing constriction to her chest.

'My...confrontation with my father happened in the open-plan offices of Jacob Holdings. Someone snapped a photo. The next thing I know, the whole humiliating business is splashed online, as if our sordid, fucked-up family drama is entertainment.'

Her lungs seized. He'd left New York to get away from his personal life and that of his parents' divorce being played out like a soap opera on the internet?

He jerked his chin. 'It was my fault. I hurt my mother. I should have spoken to Hal in private. When he confessed his...affair, I acted hot, without thinking, and I caused her pain. Humiliation.'

'It wasn't your fault.' Her voice croaked past her scratchy throat.

He shook his head, nostrils flared. 'It's one thing to be betrayed by someone who's supposed to love you. It's another entirely to watch that devastation play out publicly, everyone judging, commenting, whispering.' His lip curled.

Essie's head spun. How could she tell him she'd used the amazing, no-strings sex between them as fodder for her blog? Poor, affection-starved, sex-starved Essie had cast aside her principles for a taste of success—the heady feeling of being taken seriously.

They'd travelled deep into the Oxfordshire countryside by now. Essie stared at the hedgerows without seeing the beauty, her mind churning in time with her stomach. Why had she been so impetuous? So irresponsible? Not only had she treated the man she'd come to know and to care for like a...like an object, she had no doubt Ash could slap her with a lawsuit that would blow her beloved blog and any future career as a clinical psychologist out of existence.

Should she tell him now about *Illegally Hot*?

He'd hate her. He'd call things off.

What if her poorly timed confession ruined the wedding? Harley deserved her big day. And his mother was flying in...

Hello, my name's Essie. I shagged your son and then used the experience to flavour my online career...

What if she lost Ben and Ash in one fell swoop? She'd only have herself to blame.

As the silent miles passed, Ash lost to his thoughts, Essie to hers, she made a vow. A reckoning of her own making was heading her way. All she had to do was choose the right moment to explain to this amazing man why she'd done what she'd done.

Piece of wedding cake.

CHAPTER TEN

HE DESERVED A damned medal. He'd spent the entire afternoon and evening with a fake smile plastered on his face, walked his sister down the aisle and kept his opinions to himself, when all he wanted to do was drag Harley aside and beg her to reconsider her rash decision. He couldn't deny the ceremony, under a rose-clad arbour, had been touching. And Harley looked so happy—even he'd had a lump in his throat, especially when he'd glanced sideways at a stunning Essie and seen her pretty eyes shining with emotion.

And he was man enough to accept that his feelings were about *him*. His issues. Nothing to do with Harley and Jack, who'd had the wedding they'd wanted today—intimate, full of laughter and in exquisite surroundings.

But he couldn't shake his demons.

His mother, too, looked beautiful, but her face was drawn and pale. She'd lost weight in the weeks since he'd left New York. It couldn't be easy for her being here alone at her daughter's wedding, her brave face fooling no one. And he'd left her behind to deal with the fallout of her rotten marriage. To deal with the public speculation. To deal with his shame.

Ash looked out across the gently sloping vineyards from the terrace where he'd detoured after a trip to bathroom. He sucked in air that felt too thin and willed his stray emotions back under control.

This whole fucking wedding thing had unsettled him anew. Not because he was still hung up on the ex not worth his consideration, but because Essie's gentle probing over the last few days and his cathartic confessions had thrown up comparisons, ones between him then and him now, and the evidence was growing increasingly hard to bury.

He'd struggled to answer Essie's questions about love, because the truth was he could hand on heart admit that he probably hadn't loved his fiancée. Not the way he should have. The way Essie described with her fun facts and scientific evidence. No wonder his ex had looked elsewhere.

And it wasn't the loss of that imagined love that had hurt so much. It wasn't even the lies, the deception. What hurt the most was that he'd handed over control of his happiness to those unworthy of it. He'd held himself back for so long after Maggie, believing the worst, something he never wanted to experience again.

All he'd done was live a half-life in between and then hurt others in his frustration with himself, his mother in particular.

Perhaps he was incapable of the kind of love Essie described. A chip off the old block. As ruthless, selfish and incapable of a meaningful, honest relationship as Hal Jacob. Genetics must count for something. But would he ever know if he refused to even consider the possibility?

Essie.

She was so open, so honest and so giving. Way too good for him with his issues and his rigid rules and his impenetrable guard.

Ash spun towards the festivities. He'd left her alone for too long. Not that he could claim her as his date, but, between him and Ben, they'd managed to keep both of their single sisters occupied on the dance floor all evening.

He re-entered the conservatory, his stare scanning for her. Her ready touch was the only thing to ease his restlessness. Her bright smile. And her dirty laugh. Even her fun facts.

The way she looked up at him. The way she embraced their chemistry with her cheeky sense of humour and her quirky logic. The way she commanded her femininity with grace and steely determination, and a massive heart.

He found her talking with Ben at the edge of the makeshift dance floor. The happy couple and Alex and Libby slow danced under the twinkle of a thousand lights.

Ben saw Ash approach and lifted his chin in greeting before kissing Essie's cheek and heading towards the hotel's main foyer.

Her porcelain skin glowed pale under the lights and her eyes peeled back his layers, leaving him raw and more conflicted than ever.

'Are you okay?' She stepped closer, her stare flicking to the dance floor before settling back on his.

Ash threw caution to the wind and curved his hand over her hip. He hated that he couldn't touch her when he wanted to. Hated that he'd left it to Harley to introduce her to his mother as 'Ben's sister'. Hated that the past he couldn't let go, his hang-ups, had placed a filter across her pretty eyes.

'I'm fine. Are you having fun?'

She nodded. Her hand brushed his, fingers lingering for a second. 'You don't look fine.'

He couldn't fool her. 'I'm just worried about my mother—she's lost a little weight. I feel responsible.'

Ash guided her to a chair and took the one opposite. Her small frown and worry-etched eyes slayed him. He shouldn't have said anything. Should have allowed her to enjoy the festivities while he attended his pity party, solo.

He clasped both her hands in his while his mind raced with all the ways he'd been an idiot.

'Have you talked it through with her? I'm sure she doesn't hold you responsible.'

'She doesn't, but being the messenger of doom sucks whichever way you look at it. I can never take it back, or undo the pain.'

'But you were right. Better she heard it from you than someone else.' She paled and looked away. 'I feel guilty...about Ben.' Her teeth pulled at her lip. 'Don't look at me like that.' She stared at her lap, where her hands clenched.

He spoke softly, too uncertain of his own thoughts, motivations and emotions. 'How am I looking at you?' How did he feel about her revelation?

'Like you expect my brother to march you to the nearest church with a shotgun aimed between your shoulder blades.' She was too perceptive. Saw him way too clearly.

'I—'

Had their secret-keeping days come to an end? A natural conclusion? Her limpid eyes lanced him, and he wanted to wrap her in his arms, to carry her out of here and kiss her until she looked at him as she'd done on Saturday night after their shower.

'Why don't we talk about it when we're back in London?' It was about time he manned up. Came clean with Ben. It was his responsibility. He hadn't been able to keep his hands off her, despite his damned pathetic rules. Perhaps if he ended things now, he could go to Ben in all honesty and say, 'It happened, but it's over.'

His guts twisted with eye-watering force.

The thought of going back to being friends with Essie, or even acquaintances, left him more impotent and off balance than when he'd sweated his way down the aisle this afternoon with his sister on his arm and a hundred different divorce scenarios in his head.

But Essie deserved a full relationship with her brother. He wouldn't stand in the way.

She looked over his shoulder to where Harley, Hannah and Jack were huddled around Hannah's phone laughing, probably at some atrocious selfie. 'You have a great family. Aside from my mum, Ben's all I have.'

Ash's chest grew tighter and tighter. Telling Ben about them would shift things between him and Essie far outside the realms of fun. But if he was honest he'd lost his precious control of this attraction days ago.

Fight for her.

Where the fuck had that come from?

She looked wearier than he'd ever seen her. He'd underestimated the toll this had all taken on her, or he'd seen it but ignored it because he was selfish and wanted her still. He cupped her cheek. 'Why don't you head upstairs? Take a bath? Things are pretty much over here. Just some mushy shit going on over there.' He jerked his head back in the direction of his sappy sisters, who were a bit tipsy and had sandwiched Jack between them on the dance floor for one last slow dance.

She nodded, her eyes glassy as she stared at their entwined fingers in her lap. And then she shook it off, her expression brightening as she watched the twin sandwich on display. 'Fun fact—did you know that simply holding hands with the person you love can alleviate pain and fear and reduce stress? It's the oxytocin the brain releases.'

He nodded, his throat so damned tight he had to loosen his collar. 'I'll tell the happy couple.'

She stood, glancing over at the dance floor. 'I think they know.' She smiled down at him, the saddest smile he'd ever seen, before she turned to leave.

He halted her retreat. 'Don't worry about Ben.'

She shook her head. 'Don't worry about your mum.'

She left him floundering at the centre of the monumental mess he'd made.

Ash tapped gently on the door to Essie's hotel room, his eyes scanning the corridor. He had no explanation for why he stood at her door at one a.m., for any of the wedding party who might spot him. He just knew a team of wild horses couldn't keep him away.

If this was to be their last night before he confronted Ben tomorrow, he just had to kiss her one last time. Hold her once more. See the rapture on her face as they shared one last intimacy. Somehow, between the fun facts and the fun sex, she'd worked her way under his skin. All of her—her beauty, her vulnerabilities, her thirst for new experiences.

The door flew open and there she stood, dressed in a baggy, oversized T-shirt that hung from one shoulder, her long, pale legs leading to the views of nirvana he knew were underneath. He had no right to touch her—he never had—but he wanted her anyway. With the same ferocity of need he'd experienced since the day they'd met.

How had he ever imagined himself immune to her? He was a fool and it was too late for a vaccine.

'Invite me in.' He tried to temper the gruffness from his voice, but he craved her so badly he could hardly draw breath. Perhaps it was the promise of one last time. But however he looked at it, he couldn't stay away. And he suspected it was simply Essie herself that drove his uncontrollable need. A need he'd have to quash soon.

Unless you keep her.

Fuck. She wasn't a possession. And she deserved way more than a commitment-phobic, cynical asshole like him. She deserved her happily-ever-after—the whole cake, not just the crumbs. Her scientific love. And he was the last man qualified to give her that.

But he could give her the only thing he'd ever given her.

A fun time. A new experience.

Why did it sound so empty? Hollow? Pathetic?

She held the door open and he stepped inside. As soon as she'd shut it behind him, she turned to face him. 'I need to talk to—'

Ash pressed his fingers over her soft lips. 'I know

what you need. What we both need.' He'd made his decision to talk to Ben. The mess he'd made of his personal life was old news and he'd be damned if he spent what little remaining time he had left with her trawling through his issues.

He might not be the man for her long term, but he could show her how rare and precious she was, and what she did to him and, hopefully, when they parted, she would feel her own worth and have nothing to regret.

She nodded, her breathtaking face lifted to his as he dragged her close with one arm banded around her waist and slanted his mouth over hers. Her soft lips parted under his with a sigh. As always, she embraced what they shared, never once pressing him for labels, or more than he could offer.

Did anyone deserve a woman as amazing as Essie?

Ash bunched the hem of her shirt in his fists and lifted it over her head, breaking from their kiss for the split second it took to dispense with the garment and slide his stare over her magnificent nakedness. He scooped his arms around her waist, hoisting her from her feet and stumbling backwards towards the bed so she sprawled over him, covering him from chest to thigh in a tumble of naked limbs and a cloud of Essie-scented hair.

Ash filled his lungs and his hands with her, memorising every nuance of this unique woman. With every passing beat, her kisses grew more desperate, the breathy moans in her throat more frantic and her fingers more insistent. And her ardour matched his.

Ash rolled them so she lay under him, her writhing body urging him on. She tugged at his shirt and he helped her, yanking it up from behind his head and tossing it aside.

Skin to warm skin.

Ash gripped one of her thighs, pushing her open to slot his hips in between. He captured one pink-tipped nipple, laving and lapping until she bucked in his arms and tugged at his hair, the wild, demanding side of her never far from the surface. His kisses followed the bumps of her ribs, the dip of her navel and the hollows beneath her hip bones.

He slid to the floor, tugging her ass to the edge of the bed until he was satisfied with her position. He spread her open, his gaze devouring every perfect pink inch of her.

Just one more taste.

He pressed a kiss to each thigh and then he leaned in to touch the tip of his tongue to her clit.

She sucked in a gasp, her hands fisting the bedspread. 'Ash…'

He pulled back, a rock the size of the Isle of Wight lodged in his chest. 'Say it again. Say my name.' Some base part of him needed to hear her call out for him, to know that he wasn't alone with his unrest. To know that she saw him and only him.

She nodded and he dived once more for the slick haven between her thighs. 'Ash…' She resumed her chant, his name over and over again, while he licked and flicked and suckled.

Every time she spoke his name, his fingers clung to her thighs with a fraction more force, as if he wanted to stamp his presence all over her from head to toe, leaving no doubt. He pushed the crazy idea aside, fo-

cussing on the catches in her throat as he forced her
higher and higher.

She wasn't his.

'Yes…Ash…I'm close.' Her thighs juddered against
his face and he ceased his efforts. He wanted to be
inside her when she came, her muscles gripping him
like a fist as she wailed his name for the last time.

She cried out, but when he tore into his fly, shoving his pants down with impatient jerks and pulling
a condom from the pocket, she helped him, pushing
at the denim and sliding her hands up and down the
backs of his thighs.

Ash gripped the foil between his teeth and then
covered himself. He shucked the jeans with a kick.
Gripping her hips, he tilted her ass from the bed and
plunged inside her with one thrust. Her body welcomed him, warm and tight and as close to perfect
as he'd ever experienced.

He held himself still, allowing her to grow accus-
tomed to him inside her and allowing him time to
breathe around the block of concrete where his lungs
should be. Ash held her stare while their chests heaved
in unison, the patter of her heartbeat strong and rapid
against his chest.

'Ash…' She sighed, her fingers dancing over his
back, his shoulders and across his chest. He gipped
one wandering hand, his fingers interlocking with
hers while he pressed it to the mattress, and then followed suit with the other hand.

Her touching him with tender fingertips, while
looking at him the way she was…it was too much.
Too close to something he'd forsaken for good. Too

raw a reminder that, one day, some other lucky bastard would be gifted this woman's love.

He rocked into her, his thrusts growing in speed and power as if he was chasing down his demons. Every time he slammed home a tiny gasp left her throat. It was a sound he'd remember his whole life. Her wide eyes clung to him as if begging. Only, he was the one who should be on his knees. Worshipping.

Her breasts jiggled, desperate for his tongue, but he'd reached the point of no return, reached his limit. He released one of her hands to scoop her thigh higher until it curved over his hip. Holding it there, he sank lower, the last inch into her tight heat.

'Yes...Ash...that's—' She never finished the sentence. Her orgasm struck, her head stretched back as she gasped a prolonged wail and clamped down on him so hard, he almost closed his eyes in ecstasy. But then he'd have missed her riding out her climax with her beautiful stare on him, her swollen mouth slack as her moans petered into pants.

His head swam as oxygen deprivation sucked him under.

'Ash.' She cupped his face, pressing her mouth to his.

He collapsed forward as fire raced along his spine and down the length of his cock. He buried his face in her neck as he ground his hips through the last of the spasms. He wasn't gentle. His facial hair would mark her, but he needed a minute to flounder in private from the purging flood of emotions he daredn't name. A minute to swallow the incredible high she'd often told him existed. He crushed her beneath him while he reeled, spent, panting and completely mindfucked.

Essie ran her fingers through his hair, her soft lips pressing kisses to his temples, his ear, the side of his neck. The see-sawing of his chest dwindled away until he struggled to suck even one molecule of air past his tight throat. His scalp prickled and the sheen of sweat on his skin turned icy cold.

He shifted, gently withdrew from her languid embrace and shuffled to the en-suite to dispose of the condom. He couldn't bring himself to look in the mirror while he washed his hands. He knew what he'd see. A stupid fuck who'd broken his number one rule in life and was now paying the ultimate price. The only thing he'd had to avoid and he'd gone and done it anyway.

His best friend's sister. A wonderful woman he couldn't have and didn't deserve. A woman professionally obsessed with relationships and romantic love—two things he sucked at and had spent years forsaking. A woman who deserved a man to love her one hundred and ten per cent. To be all in. To worship her and leave her in no doubt that she was his number one priority.

No way could fucked-up Ash be that man.

Keeping his gaze averted, he returned to the bedroom to find Essie wrapped in a white sheet, her face peaceful in sleep.

Indulging in one last, ill-advised move, he slipped into the bed beside her and fell asleep with her perfectly slotted into his arms.

CHAPTER ELEVEN

THE INSISTENT VIBRATION of a phone alert woke him. Ash opened his eyes to find the bed empty beside him and the sound of the shower from the en-suite bathroom. His body stirred fully awake at the idea of joining a wet Essie.

As he slid from the bed, Essie's phone vibrated again. He flipped it over and placed it on the nightstand, pausing when the screen lit up to reveal the string of notifications, which had sent the device into an early-morning frenzy.

You have fifty-three comments

What the…?

Ash's stomach pitched. Since his own brush with the gossip columns and the subsequent social media roasting around the story of one of New York's most influential families crumbling in the most sordid way, he'd deleted his own accounts.

Was Essie victim to a similar backlash? No, why would she be a target? Unless it was something to do with him…

Perhaps the gossip rags had caught wind of Harley's rushed, closed-door wedding. Perhaps they'd somehow acquired the limited guest list and sought a comment or a photo from Essie.

His scalp prickled even as he swiped his thumb over the screen.

It wasn't locked.

Every nerve in his body fired as he snooped—as soon as he'd verified that the messy, dirty Jacob drama hadn't spread to include Essie, he'd stop reading.

It took several beats for Ash to understand the content displayed on her phone. A blog.

Relationships and Other Science Experiments

So this was her little secret. Not quite an agony aunt. His mouth twitched at her sense of humour and her conversational writing style. He read on for a few lines, the latest post unsurprisingly one about the inexhaustible romance of weddings and the hidden tangle of complex relationships at play when extended families met, often for the first time in years.

One phrase, repeated in the comments at the bottom of the post, leapt from the screen and smacked him between the eyes. *Illegally Hot.*

Whatever it referred to, Essie's fans wanted more.

He shouldn't pry. No good ever came from snooping. But some unseen demon controlled his fingers, which scrolled the screen in search of earlier posts.

A familiar photo—the view of the London Eye taken from St James's Park. The photo he'd taken for her the day they'd met.

With each line he read, wave after wave of heat

flooded his body until his fists clenched and his jaw ached.

She'd written about their one-night stand. About their shock meeting the next day. About some arrogant asshole who'd rocked her world, but had the emotional intelligence of a rock.

He was paraphrasing, but one thing was glaringly obvious. *He* was *Illegally Hot*. And Essie had used him as tawdry inspiration fodder for her online musings. Exposing his hang-ups in a public forum…for humour…for entertainment… To humiliate him? To laugh behind his back?

No wonder the damned phone was never far from her hand. And every ping, every muted vibration represented someone new reading about or commenting on his sex life…

Ash tossed the phone on the nightstand, his stomach rigid as he sucked in a breath laced with razor blades. She'd put their relationship on the internet. For anyone to see? And kept it from him? All this time? While he'd agonised over the rights and wrongs of his attraction to her. All these weeks she'd made a fool of him…been laughing at him… Did everyone know? The Yard's staff? Ben?

His gut ached as if he'd taken a knee to the balls. He needed to get out of here.

Essie appeared in that moment, her open smile sliding from her face as she took in his posture. He stood, silently tugging on his boxers and his shirt—he was exposed enough.

'*Illegally Hot?* Did you come up with that all by yourself?'

Wrapped in a towel, her hair wet, she hovered,

breathtaking but paralysed, on the threshold. His vision tunnelled as he clamped his jaw shut and turned away from her to find his jeans.

She gasped, paling. 'Ash, I'm sorry, I—'

'You're fucking sorry? Is that all you have? Not quite your usual level of eloquence. Or is that reserved for your tacky sexploits?'

She moved towards him, a small anguished squeak leaving her throat. His outstretched hand stopped her dead in her tracks. If she touched him now, he might actually hurl, so tightly knotted were his intestines.

'Is everything entertainment to you? People's emotions? Their challenges? Their...pain.' What a fool he'd been. Again. He'd told her about his fiancée, his parents, his guilt over his mother... Would he read all about it online soon? Another science experiment?

How had he, only hours ago, imagined himself developing feelings for her? He didn't know her at all. Not this manipulative, deceptive version she'd hidden so successfully behind the bubbly, ingenuous, emotionally damaged exterior.

'I never meant to hurt you.'

Fuck, that sentiment sucked. 'So said every selfish person who ever acted in their own interest and only considered the consequences when they were found out.' Ash yanked on his jeans and scooped his own phone and the key to his room from the desk.

'Don't go. I can explain.'

'I don't give a fuck about your explanation. You used me. Not for one second did you consider my feelings before you published that crap—' he pointed at the nightstand and the offending device '—for anyone to read.'

'Ash…' She stepped closer, sucking the oxygen from the enclosed space until Ash's lungs recoiled. 'It was meant to be funny… I didn't name you.'

He snorted, expecting to see plumes of fire coming from his nostrils. 'Do you know why my family drama, my parents' split, was such salacious gossip, the kind you find funny?' He loomed over her, his chest working hard to oxygenate his blood before his head exploded. 'The juicy little details? The irresistible intrusion into our personal lives…all in the name of fair-game entertainment for the masses?'

Essie had the good grace to pale almost white and stay silent, a tiny shake of her head her only answer.

'The woman at the centre of the row between Hal and me, the final intolerable insult to my mother, the woman he confessed to fucking in front of my entire workplace, was *my* ex-fiancée.'

Her jaw dropped, and she swayed unsteadily on her feet, but it gave him no satisfaction.

Ash marched to the door, turning to cast one final look at the woman he'd almost trusted. Almost…

No.

'Forgive me if I have no intention of becoming a public laughing stock again.'

The door slammed behind him with a whoosh of air, blocking Essie's startled image from view.

Ash slapped his hand over the stop button on the treadmill in his apartment's fully equipped gym and wiped sweat from his eyes with a towel. He'd arrived home from Oxfordshire three hours ago, but he hadn't been able to quench the fire burning inside him any other way. Even now, after a solid hour of relentless pounding, when his noodle-like legs threatened to give out at any stage, the flames still licked at him—burning, taunting and mocking. Because he craved her still, when the taste of her betrayal should have turned his stomach for good.

Stupid fuck.

How could he have been so dumb? So taken in by her seeming ingenuousness and English-rose charm? When all the time she wielded a poisonous pen…or a noxious keyboard.

Of course he'd been right not to trust her. He'd been here before. Twice. Once with the lies his fiancée had told to keep her true affair with his father a secret, and once when Hal had finally tossed out the truth in a fit of malice for anyone at Jacob Holdings to hear.

Only this time, the pain slashed deeper, the wound gaping open. He'd thought she was different. He'd thought he'd learned his lesson and done everything in his power to protect himself.

Well, there was one more thing he could do. This time, he wasn't going down without a fight. He was done. Done with humiliation, done with being the last to know. Ash stumbled from the treadmill and eyed his phone where he'd switched it to silent. His fingers curled into his palm.

He wouldn't check.

How close he'd come to…feeling emotions that left him wanting to build barricades to protect himself! He needed fortifications more than ever, to protect himself from the feelings he'd realised last night were as foreign as the adopted country he'd chosen. Because whatever he'd felt for his ex, it paled in comparison to the unstoppable wave building in him now. He should never have let things go so far—caring for her hadn't been part of the plan.

A yell from his living room sucked him to his senses.

Ben stood framed in the doorway, his face slightly haggard with questions burning in his eyes. Ash had known this reckoning was coming, and yet he still recoiled. Telling your friend you'd slept with his sister was one thing. Telling him you'd allowed yourself to be duped, humiliated by not just one woman, but two...

Ash stalked to the kitchen with Ben trailing. He held out his arm, offering Ben a seat, and retrieved two bottles of beer from the fridge. 'What did she tell you?'

Is she okay?

No.

There'd be no asking about Essie, thinking about Essie and certainly no going to Essie.

'That it happened. That it was over.' Ben collapsed onto a bar stool, and accepted the beer Ash handed him. 'What did you do to her?'

Ash deserved the accusation in his friend's stare. He should never have slept with her after the first time. He had no defence. Never a good position for an attorney. But she wasn't blameless here. 'I met her the day before you left for New York. I didn't know who she was the first time.'

Fuck, that sounded all wrong.

Ben stared for long challenging seconds. 'I know Maggie hurt you and that you only do casual.' Ben gripped the bottle, his knuckles white. 'So why would you lead Essie on like that?'

Fuck, he didn't want to do this now, but there was no escape. 'We were just fooling around. She said she wanted the same thing. I should have told you.'

Ben paled even more, his lips thin and white. 'And now? You're done and she clearly wanted more because she's broken-hearted.' Ben speared his fingers through his hair. 'I offered her the job so I could get to know her, to make amends for the shit our father pulled. She's sweet and kind and fun. She's so desperate for approval...'

Ash nodded. It couldn't have been easy for Ben to find out he had a sister, either. A massive adjustment. 'I didn't know about your father, I'm sorry.'

Ben swallowed, his face twisted as he shook his head. 'Fuck... She's been treated so fucking shabbily by men, men who are supposed to care about her and love her and protect her, part of her believes she's unworthy of a decent relationship.' Ben took a swig of beer, wiping his mouth with the back of his hand. 'Please tell me you didn't take advantage of that.'

Had he? Had he unknowingly taken her fears and insecurities and used them for his own ends? He'd known Essie had a poor relationship with her and Ben's father, something Ash could relate to. Did she crave what she'd never had? Did she want it with him?

It didn't matter. It was too late. Over.

'If I did it was unintentional.' Ash ground his teeth together, willing truth into them—he'd told her his position from the start. But as he'd learned more about her, a part of him had known he would hurt her. He just hadn't guessed she'd hurt him in return.

Ben ignored his plea, as if lost to his own turmoil over his sister. 'He was never there for her. He kept me and his wife a secret from her until she discovered his lies by accident. Fuck. She deserves better than him.'

Acid flooded the back of Ash's throat. 'I agree. But she's not blameless in this.' He should leave it alone. Accept all the responsibility. But those fingers of mistrust still burrowed into his brain.

Ben stared. 'What does that mean?'

'Did you know about her blog?' The heat returned, scalding, diminishing.

Ben frowned. 'Not until today, but what does that have to do with anything?'

The words trapped in his throat, covered in barbed wire. 'She's…been writing about us. About me.'

'So? She mentioned something… What's the big deal?'

'Aside from the fact I don't enjoy reading about my private life, my sex life on the internet…?'

Ben shrugged, eyes darting.

Ash took a seat at the kitchen bench, next to Ben. 'Did you…catch up on any gossip while you were in New York?'

'What the…? You know that's not my style. What does this have to do with Essie?'

Damn, the words stuck deep down in his gullet. 'Remember when…Maggie…called off the wedding?'

Ben nodded, one hand scraping over his haggard face.

Ash gulped beer, the cool liquid soothing his parched throat. 'Turned out the affair was a cover. Some scapegoat schmuck. She was really fucking Hal.'

Ben sputtered. 'Bullshit.'

Ash stared straight ahead. He couldn't witness whatever expression his friend wore for fear the humiliation would burrow into him so deep, he'd need a lobotomy to excise it. 'It's true. I didn't know it at the time, but Hal took great pleasure in informing me in front of a whole office of Jacob Holdings staff.'

Several beats passed. The occasional swallow of beer the only sound. 'Word spread. Before I knew it, the gossip rags were speculating on the demise of my parents' marriage, whether my playboy reputation would be damaged or enhanced and how destructive it would be to Jacob Holdings stock.' He faced his friend. 'That's why I came to London. I couldn't go back to work for Hal. I had paps chasing me down the street and, having created the mess, I had to rush to tell my mother before she heard of it at the gym or the grocery store.'

Ben shook his head, shock rendering him slack-jawed. 'I didn't know.'

Ash snorted. 'You and me both.'

'Does Essie know?'

Ash nodded.

They sat in silence. Then Ben said, 'She's sorry for what she did. Perhaps if you talked to her...'

Ash shook his head. He would. But not tonight.

'I think she's in love with you.'

No.

Ash couldn't deny they'd had chemistry from the start. And yes, she'd slipped under his guard, blindsided him with her honest and refreshing outlook on the world, her ethereal beauty and her bubbly personality. But not love.

Ben glanced at his watch. 'I have to be at the club.'

Ash jutted his chin in silence. Where did these events leave him and Ben? Would he survive bumping into Essie down the track? She'd always be a part of Ben's life, quite rightly.

At the door, Ben turned. 'Ash. I'm sorry, man.'

Ash nodded. 'Me, too.'

And then he was alone again with only his restlessness for company.

Essie stacked the last chair into place and stretched out her aching back muscles. The basement club had been booked out for a private function that night—a fashion show and corporate party. The removal crew would arrive first thing to dismantle the temporary runway and extra seating.

The last place she'd wanted to be tonight was here with her happy face plastered on and the requisite nothing-is-too-much-trouble attitude, but she'd promised Ben she'd lock up the club, and in reality she'd rather have been here with the noise and the bodies than home alone with her self-recriminations.

Riding back to London earlier with Ben, she'd found hiding her desolation from her brother impossible. He'd coaxed the whole tale from her, his bunched jaw the only sign of any judgment. To his credit, he'd been supportive and understanding, something she didn't deserve for her role in hurting Ash, her own guilt a sharp blade slicing deep.

Flicking off the lights, she made her way upstairs, her tired feet encased in lead.

Her stomach clenched at the memory of Ash's face. She hated what she'd done to him. How much she'd devastated him through her thoughtlessness. She'd convinced herself he couldn't be identified, so he couldn't be hurt. But in light of his shocking confession about his father and his ex…

She'd betrayed his trust.

Humiliated him.

All because she'd been overwhelmed by their chemistry, in awe of the amazing sex and flushed with the heady power of holding her own in a relationship for the first time. And then later…

She only had herself to reprimand. If she'd been honest with him from the start, if she'd owned her feelings, said, 'This is who I am, take it or leave it,' instead of shoving them back inside for fear of his judgment or disapproval or indifference… He'd been honest with her from day one. He'd never once claimed to want anything beyond sex. She'd just misinterpreted his looks and his touches. She'd seen something, felt something that wasn't there. At least not for Ash.

She'd known the score going in and learned a long time ago that even when people said one thing, they usually did something else. Something that suited *them*.

But somewhere along the way, perhaps dazzled by the private jets and Paris and the glamorous clubs, she'd fooled herself into believing, just this once, she could have more. Have the real deal. An equal relationship where she was valued, cherished, respected. For once she'd ignored the loud and clear warning bells and imagined she could have someone for herself, someone who not just barely tolerated her, but actually wanted her in their life. Not an inconvenience, but as necessary as oxygen.

So the last time they'd been together in Oxfordshire had, at least for her, been way more intimate than all the previous occasions combined. She'd convinced herself they could be making love, not just banging each other. That didn't mean Ash had felt the same. She understood his anger, but could he run away so quickly if he shared one iota of her feelings?

Gnawing at her lip, she swung through the staff-only door. Yet again, she'd learned the hard way that relationships were fine in theory, the black-and-white science irrefutable, but disastrous in reality. She was an expert in one, but definitely a novice at the other. Nothing had changed. Only, this lesson carried a permanency that rolled her stomach and left her empty.

Bereft.

She slammed to a halt, her small gasp catching in her throat.

Ash stood in her office.

He wore running gear, his shirt dark with sweat as if he'd sprinted all the way with his backside on fire.

Perhaps sensing her behind him, he lifted his stare from a white envelope on her otherwise clear desk.

Essie's knees threatened to give way.

He was here.

To see her?

'Ash—'

'I came to deliver this. I…I assumed everyone had gone home.' He looked away and another part of Essie cracked and crumbled.

'I'm sorry. Please let me explain.' The words tumbled out in a rush.

Ash collected the envelope from the desk and Essie

spotted her name. He lanced her with a cold stare. 'Will your apology change the outcome? The facts?'

'No, but... Please...'

At his silence she ploughed on, certain he'd never forgive her, but desperate to have him understand. 'I didn't think I'd see you again after that first night. And then the next day you were my boss.' She lifted her gaze to his. 'I'd never had a one-night stand before. I...it made a good cautionary tale. Careful who you sleep with—it might turn out to be your boss.' Her voice trailed away with the ice of his stare.

She should have told him sooner. She'd been about to the night of the wedding. And then he'd looked at her as if he'd wanted more than sex and she'd succumbed, desperate to know if his feelings in any way matched hers.

'Yes, I can see that. Very entertaining.' He tapped the letter against his palm, his face an expressionless mask. His damp T-shirt clung to his ripped chest. If she hadn't needed every spare lick of saliva to lubricate her tight throat, she'd have drooled down her front.

'Ash, it wasn't like that. I never named you or wrote anything identifiable. And I didn't know about your... past—I would never hurt you like that. Only you know I was writing about us, well...just the incredible sex. I finally saw what all the fuss was about.'

Her excuses sounded all wrong. Her writing was exposition, scientific theory and a dash of poetic licence.

'I'm sure you didn't mean to be discovered. But lies grow. They twist and mutate and sprout claws. I could identify myself.' He thrust the envelope at her. 'I have a professional reputation. We fucked. That's it.'

Essie winced as if he'd slapped her.

'I don't want my sexual prowess to become a topic of public speculation. I'll be a laughing stock. I won't tolerate that again.'

'Ash. I understand you're angry with me.' She was furious with herself.

He pointed at the envelope trembling in her hand. 'Consider yourself severed. You can kiss your precious blog goodbye. Perhaps you'll be forced to sell out, practise what you preach, pedal your psychobabble for actual paying customers. You're about to find out the hard way, you can't hide behind theory for ever.'

'You...you're suing me? But—'

He stalked closer, pinning her with his steely glare.

Breathing became harder. His cold eyes flicked south to her mouth and then back again, the ice thawing. Or perhaps it was just her imagination. Just wishful thinking.

She pressed her back to the door, her palms flat to stop herself reaching for him. If he recoiled from her touch, backed away, she wouldn't survive.

This time her voice emerged a whisper. 'I'm sorry. Please let me explain.'

He was so close now his warm breath tickled her lips.

'My father was never there. Growing up, I would try to remember things I wanted to tell him, little things. I started writing them down until the next time he came home. And then later when I knew the truth, I used my blog to process my feelings. Writing about you was a lapse, a mistake—one I won't make again.'

If she took a deep breath, her nipples would brush

his chest. But she couldn't even draw in enough air to stop her head spinning.

He'd listened patiently but now he snarled. 'Well, some of us don't have that luxury—we have to deal, internalise, without publicly splurging every one of our feelings. Do you think you're the only person with a shitty father figure?'

'Of course not. I—'

'Oh, spare me your pity.' The pain in his eyes stole the last of her oxygen.

If she hadn't been leaning against the door, her legs would have given way. How could someone do that to their own son? She'd thought Frank was bad enough. No wonder Ash had fled from his life in search of a fresh start. And all she'd done was confirm his beliefs that he was right not to trust anyone.

'I understand that. But I was blindsided by our chemistry. I'd never experienced anything like it. For the first time in my life, I had some power in a relationship. It was heady, wonderful, but overwhelming. For the first time, I didn't feel worthless, and then when people liked what I wrote...I got professional validation, too. I messed up with the blog. I should have told you. I was trying to tell you the night of Harley's wedding.'

He placed one hand on the door above her shoulder and leaned close. At first she was certain he planned to kiss her, the heat in his eyes, the small catch of his breath, the way the tip of his tongue touched his top lip for a split second.

But then he must have changed his mind. He made eye contact and Essie shivered.

'I was right not to trust you.'

He wasn't listening. He'd shut down already. She'd done the damage and missed the opportunity to make it right.

He backed off as suddenly as if they'd been interrupted in an illicit, forbidden kiss. Essie's bones rattled from the icy chills of his frosty brush-off. That he could deliver such a blow without a flicker of emotion told her he'd be a formidable opponent in the courtroom. Something she hoped she'd never have to witness or experience, despite the legal document clutched in her hand.

'Ash, I humiliated you in a moment of stupid impulsiveness and I regret it.'

It was the now or never moment. Mustering every shred of her courage, she pressed herself back against the opened door to gain another sliver of space from his derision. 'But I kept the secret from you because I...I started to realise...I love you, and I didn't want anything to ruin that.'

Silence.

His cold stare remained unchanged.

Essie hovered for long, torturous, doubt-filled seconds. When he didn't move, didn't speak, she stumbled away, blindly barging through the exit and out into the night.

Much later, alone in a deserted Tube carriage, she looked down at the envelope still crumpled in her hand.

A bubble of hysterical laughter burst through her numbness.

How would she ever afford legal representation to fight him?

And why would she bother?

She loved him and she'd hurt him. It was time to face the consequences.

CHAPTER TWELVE

ESSIE'S TWENTY-FIFTH BIRTHDAY arrived with a predictability that left her gunning for a fight. At first, the card on the mat, addressed with an airmail sticker and recognisable handwriting, sent familiar chills down her bare arms and legs. But reading the dismissive, one-line greeting from her father fired her determination—today was the first day of the rest of her life.

A new Essie rose from the ashes. One who'd learned valuable lessons from the way she'd treated Ash. Yes, she'd hurt him and lost him—he'd already retreated behind the walls he'd constructed long ago, the defences she'd helped to refortify.

But Ash, and to some degree Ben, had taught her something. In loving Ash, she fully understood herself worthy of love in return. She wanted his love, even though she could survive without it. She had all the theory, and now the confidence in her ability to practise and live an authentic life. Not sit and wait for the scraps others tossed her way.

She took the annual cheque—her father's way of appeasing his own demons for his life choices and one she'd resolutely rejected since her fifteenth birthday—

and tore it in two. With the birthday ritual complete, she dropped both halves and the card into the bin, donned her sunglasses and left for the Tube station, her step lighter.

Half an hour later she waltzed into The Yard to find Ben and Ash drinking coffee together at the bar.

Her feet stalled for a brief second as Ash's eyes landed on her. She'd wronged him, hurt him in the worst way. He might not be able to love her in return, but she was done apologising for loving him.

'Good. You're both here. I need to speak to you.' Essie stood before them, clutching the straps of her backpack.

Two sets of wide, wary eyes followed her—one so like her own, her insides trembled—and what she'd come to say clogged in her throat. The other so blue, she imagined she could see inside Ash, to his deepest darkest fears. And maybe she could. Maybe she'd always been able to. But she couldn't see what she wanted to see.

She'd messed up, but she'd survive.

All humans shared the same basic longings— safety, love, acceptance. She deserved those things and so did Ash. But it was too late for him to find them with her. She'd ruined what tiny chance they'd had.

Essie turned her burning eyes away from Ash and focussed on her brother, her chin lifted. Slipping the backpack from her shoulder, she retrieved the letter she'd composed at six a.m. this morning after writing her latest blog post on the importance of self-love, self-acceptance and self-forgiveness, and handed it over to a puzzled Ben.

She cleared her throat. 'I'm handing in my notice.'

Ben took the envelope with a wince. Essie ploughed on—she needed to get all she wanted to say out, before emotion paralysed her vocal cords. Because she was done being needy. Done waiting for other people's approval. Done with scientific theory.

She would survive the practice and emerge improved, wiser, unstoppable.

Her bruised heart would heal eventually.

Essie cleared her throat. 'As we only had a verbal contract, I won't be working that notice, but you'll be fine without me.' Ash could wax lyrical on the ins and out of employment law as long as he liked. They wouldn't force her to stay. And Ben didn't really need her. His clubs were well-oiled machines. She suspected he'd offered her the job as some sort of olive branch, and she loved that he'd tried to make amends for their father.

'I know you only employed me because you somehow felt responsible for what Frank did. But there's no need. If you're short-staffed, I recommend promoting Josh to my position as manager, until you find someone permanent. He's way more qualified than I am anyway.'

She flicked her stare to Ash, her lungs on fire and pressure building behind her eyes so she was tempted to don the sunglasses. How long would it take him to replace her in his bed? Would he even bother? Perhaps he'd go back to his lonely one-night rule. She loved him enough to want more than that for him, even when, because of her foolish actions, it couldn't be her.

'Essie,' said Ben.

She held up her hand. She needed to say everything she'd come here to say. 'Going forward, I want us to have a real relationship. We have a chance to build a lasting bond, away from the usual influences of childhood sibling rivalry. I don't resent you for getting a phone before me or being allowed to stay up later and you never had to play dress-ups with me or read me dumb stories.'

He grinned, giving her the courage to continue.

'If you want to be a part of my life like I want to be a part of yours—' her breath caught, but she sucked in air through her nostrils, fighting the burn behind her eyes '—you'll meet me halfway.'

She shrugged, her whole body buzzing with renewed energy.

Ben nodded, his eyes sliding to Ash. 'Of course I want that.' He reached for her hand and squeezed her fingers. 'But what will you do without a job?'

She squeezed back. 'I have plenty to do. I want to put more time into promoting my blog to wider audiences, and I'm thinking of writing a book. It turns out I have something valuable to say about relationships. I'm a bit of an expert in the field, actually.' She winked at him. 'You know you're damned lucky I'm your sister, don't you?'

She swung her backpack onto her shoulder and offered a beaming Ben a small smile. She loved him. Always would. But her happiness was her responsibility—no more waiting around for someone else's acceptance or approval. No more settling.

And Ash…

Her eyes stung and she blinked away the burn.

Well, that was over. She'd hurt him, and he couldn't

love her back. But she'd meant what she'd said to him last night.

Her vocal cords constricted, almost choking off her newfound bravery.

As if sensing the private moment, Ben muttered something about making an important phone call and disappeared.

Part of Essie wanted to follow him. But it was time to own her mistakes and her feelings.

His expression was closed off, wary. The last shred of hope inside her withered and died. 'I know I messed up. I'm truly sorry I hurt you and I hope one day you can forgive me.'

Her voice broke, but she smiled through the scalding heat behind her eyes. 'But more importantly, and I'm saying this because I love you and I want you to be happy, I hope one day you'll want more with someone. You deserve more.'

He swallowed, his jaw bunched. Her hand itched to touch him, to feel the silk of his hair or the scrape of his scruff. She dug her nails into her palm and looked down, her own vision swimming. 'I allowed what my father did to hold me back but I'm done with that. Don't let yours hold you back, Ash.'

With a final, slightly wobbly smile, she turned her back on the man she loved and made her way out into the sun of a new day.

'What did she say?' Ben joined Ash at the window, where he'd moved to stare after a retreating Essie.

He shrugged, his lungs too big for his chest as he grinned at his friend. 'She's magnificent, isn't she?'

Every nerve, every muscle, every impulse in him

fired, urging him to chase after her. He'd missed her beautiful, ready smile, her effervescent personality and her dirty laughter over one of her own jokes. But he'd put paid to her trust with his bastard move last night. He had no intention of suing her. He'd been angry. He'd lashed out.

Asshole.

Now he had something his friend needed to hear. 'I love her.'

Ben swivelled to face him. 'Of course you do. Dickhead.' He thumped Ash's shoulder, making his point.

Ash sighed, a wistful smile tugging his mouth. He'd been blind long enough. 'I allowed my hang-ups to cloud my judgment. You don't need me to tell you she's the best thing that ever happened to me. To both of us.'

Ben nodded, still looking a little dazed by his sister's declarations. 'What are you going to do?'

Ash retraced his steps, his restless limbs unable to stand still for a minute longer, and tossed a note on the bar to cover the coffees. 'I'm going to do what I should have done at the wedding. I'm going to fight for her.'

Ben nodded. 'You'd better not hurt my sister again.'

Ash shook his head, his mouth pulled to a grim line. 'I will. I'm a fuck-up. But she'll put me right.' He grinned. 'Just like she did you.'

Ben nodded, another incredulous smile tugging his mouth.

Ash released a long sigh. 'Now, I'm going to say the same thing to you. You'd better always be there for my woman when she needs you. You're the man of her family—time to step up.'

Eyes rounded, Ben nodded. Then he grinned.

'Looks like we both have some ground to make up.'

He reached out his hand and Ash shook on it.

'Good luck,' they said in unison.

CHAPTER THIRTEEN

ASH STEPPED INSIDE the relative gloom of the stuffy university hall, his throat so dry he'd never be able to say what he'd come here to say. He rolled his shoulders, scanning the mingling crowds for her golden hair. He'd come to present the most important closing argument of his life. No time for nerves or hesitancy.

This was what he did.

He won.

Every negotiation.

How he'd managed to fool himself he could live without her astounded him. For an intelligent man, used to getting his own way, how had he blocked his own path for so long?

He gripped the bag containing the rain boots tighter, the smell of new rubber reminding him of what was at stake. Had he waited too long? Woken up to himself too late?

He spotted her and his heart jerked out of rhythm.

A stunningly dressed Essie, as he'd never seen her before, stood not ten feet away. She wore a fitted green dress that outlined every one of her perfect curves, matching green skyscraper heels and a light smattering of make-up, which accentuated her rosy complexion and bright eyes. Her hair was loose, styled in soft waves that made his clenched fingers itch, and a formal graduation gown completed the look.

Damn, he wanted to mess her up. To peel from her the smart, professional outfit and tangle her hair while he kissed her senseless until she believed what he had to say. Believed it down to her bones. Because he meant it and he'd waited too long to tell her.

Ben caught his eye as he strode towards the siblings, his steps determined.

Essie turned at the last moment, the laughter at whatever Ben had said sliding from her exquisite face. A bubble of stilted anticipation enclosed them as the conversations around them muted into background noise.

'What's with the wellies?' said Essie, eyeing his bag. He deserved the cold shoulder after giving her that notice of legal action. But that wasn't Essie's style.

Ash pressed his lips together. Now wasn't the time for laughter. But of course she would say the thing he least expected. So full of surprises, so refreshing, so unique. His Essie.

Don't get ahead of yourself, asshole.

'If you mean these—' he held up the rain boots '—a graduation present. Congratulations, Dr Newbold.'

She eyed the spade sticking up next to the boots in silence, keeping his worthless ass on tenterhooks.

He should have come here today with champagne and flowers and a fucking brass band. But he'd got what he'd told her from day one he'd wanted—her out of his life, him out of hers.

What an idiot.

Her magnificent bravery and heartfelt declaration yesterday had been the final slap he'd needed to wake up. Ash himself acted as the only barrier standing in the way of contentment. He'd done the hard part, breaking free of his old life, free of the poisonous relationship with his father. The rest, loving Essie, was easy.

Now all he had to do was grab hold of this wonderful woman, pray she'd walk alongside him and never let go. If she'd have him.

That remained to be seen. But if forced to do this in front of this room full of gowned academics like some sappy idiot from a romantic comedy movie, he would.

Ben cleared his throat. 'I'll uh…go find your mum and get us some champagne.' With a look that said 'don't fuck this up', his friend offered them privacy.

Ash gestured Essie to accompany him to the less crowded foyer. She obliged and he followed the sway of her gorgeous ass that was unfortunately obliterated by her billowing gown.

In a deserted corner, she turned her big blue eyes on him.

'I bluffed about the lawsuit. I was angry. I'm sorry.'

The longer she looked at him, wary and hesitant, the more his intestines knotted. 'I fucked up, too.' He held her stare, willing her to hear the earnest regret in his voice. He stepped closer, taking an indulgent second to register how fantastic she smelled, how he wanted to wake up tomorrow with her scent in his hair, on his sheets, and every morning after that.

She pointed at the shovel. 'You bought me a shovel? Are we burying a corpse?'

This time he couldn't hold in the laughter. He was

messing this up. And she applied her usual quirky sense of humour to help him out.

His fingers twitched, desperate to reach out and cup her waist. To drag her closer. He eyed her full mouth, which was painted red. 'Someone once told me to consider my carbon footprint and I promised I'd plant a forest. Fun fact—did you know a flight from New York to London produces eighty-four tons of the greenhouse gas, carbon dioxide?'

She stared at him for so long, her features an unreadable mask, a countdown began in his head as if he waited for the gavel to fall.

'I know you're celebrating with your family, so I'll cut straight to my closing statement.' Not a flicker of her beautiful smile. Damn—his best lawyer humour... 'You were right. I allowed the poor way I'd dealt with my past to stand in the way of us, and I'd like you to consider taking me back.' Her lips parted a fraction.

'Now, before you send the jury out to consider, let me present my evidence.'

'Aren't you supposed to do that *before* you close?' She tilted her head.

Heat raced up his spine. She was magnificent. Keeping him on his toes, challenging him, calling him out on his bullshit. How had he been so blind for so long? How was he managing to keep his hands off her?

'Good point. The thing is, I've done a little research myself. I'm sure you know all about Sternberg's triangular theory of love?'

She shrugged, her colour heightening a fraction. 'I do.'

So far, so good.

'We definitely have the passion, or we did have, until I behaved like a douche and overreacted. We also have the intimacy down pat.' His hand cupped her waist, fingers flexing to draw her another millimetre into his space. 'Two out of three isn't bad, as the song goes.'

She didn't step away, her eyes lifting to stare him down. 'The thing is, Ash, I'm no longer willing to settle for two thirds of what I deserve.'

His groin stirred at her proximity. At her demanding her absolute dues. Fuck, if this went his way, he'd hold on tight and never let her go.

'You don't have to, because I came here today to tell you I'm completing the triangle.'

She raised one eyebrow. 'Commitment?'

He nodded, an unfettered smile taking over his face. 'I'm all in. I want you. Every second I've spent with you has been the best fun. And, unless I fuck it up, which I plan not to, I know there's more fun in our future.' He dropped the bag and reached for both her hands, holding them between their bodies. 'I love you, Essie. Is it too late?'

She stared.

The gavel clattered to the block, the harsh clap of the hardwood echoing inside his skull.

He'd blown it.

But then she jumped into his arms, her hands tugging his neck and her body pressed to his as she kissed the shock from him with the enthusiasm he'd grown to expect. This woman was incapable of half measures, one of the things he loved most about her. Her honesty. Her emotional availability. Her complete lack of artifice. What you saw was what you got. And he wanted it all.

With his arms banded around her waist, he hauled her feet from the floor, groaning into her mouth as he swung her in a circle and then lowered her and broke free.

'I messed up your lipstick.' He wiped a smudge from her chin.

'I don't care.' She laughed, smearing the rest of the colour from his lips with her fingertips. 'That was quite a statement, counsellor.'

He shrugged. 'Some things are worth fighting for. You are worth fighting for.'

He swooped on her again, his tongue delving into her mouth and his hand slipping beneath her ceremonial gown to cup her waist and press her close. She pulled back with a small sigh, her eyes slumberous with lust.

'Wanna go to a stuffy degree ceremony lunch? I guarantee it *won't* be fun.'

He nodded, warmth spreading from his chest to the tips of his fingers, which held her a little tighter.

'As long as I can peel you out of this later, Dr Newbold.' He fingered the edge of the ceremonial gown. 'Or perhaps you could keep it on. That might be fun. Ever made love in a cap and gown?'

She laughed, shaking her head. 'Call me doctor again.' She writhed in his arms, waking up the parts of him inappropriate for the setting.

'Doctor.' He nuzzled her neck.

'Counsellor, I think you've just won your case.'

'No, I've won something better—you.'

They sealed the contract with a kiss.

* * *

Essie pushed the spade into the dirt and struck a rock. The field bordering a track of mature woodland on the Oxfordshire estate owned by Alex was marked out with rows of bagged tree saplings ready for planting. 'How many more do we have to plant before that delicious lunch you promised me?'

Ash laughed. 'Well, if you want to accompany me to New York for Christmas, you have to plant this whole forest.'

Essie pouted and attacked the rock in earnest. The quicker they planted the damn trees, the quicker she could get Ash naked. She glanced over at him dressed down in jeans and a T-shirt. As mouth-watering as ever. Who cared about greenhouse gases when Ash was around?

And he was hers. Her smile made her cheeks ache. She had two new men in her life. A fully committed brother and a proper boyfriend who was in love with her...

'Fun fact,' he said. 'Couples who play together, stay together.'

She picked up the inconveniently placed rock and tossed it to land at his feet.

He shot her a look that promised thrilling retribution.

She laughed, dropped her spade and went to him, wrapping her arms around his neck and tugging him down for a kiss. 'You totally made that up.'

He laughed. 'I did. But you're not the only one with a clever fact up her sleeve, Doctor.'

She sobered. 'Well, even if it is true, you'll be practising law again soon—not much time for playing or fun.'

He scooped her from the ground and she wrapped her legs around his waist, grateful she'd worn the cut-off shorts he could never resist as she felt the prod of his erection between her legs.

'There's always time for fun.' His lips brushed hers. 'But to be certain, ever experienced living with the man you love?'

She gasped and shook her head, which spun with his question as if he'd twirled her around in a circle.

'Good. Because I think we should move in together.'

Essie wriggled free, sliding down the length of his hard body. 'Seriously?'

He nodded, wicked light glinting in his eyes.

'But you live on the wrong side of London.'

He shook his head, holding her hips still and rubbing himself against her belly. 'I'm moving. New legal practice. New apartment. New girlfriend...'

She couldn't stop the grin that made her cheeks ache. He turned serious. 'Will you live with me—somewhere we choose together?' He cupped her cheek, his fingers tangling in her hair.

She nodded, flying into his arms once more. After a kiss that turned heated enough she scoped the nearby woods for a potential spot to take things further, he placed her feet on the ground and wiped what was probably a smudge of dirt from her cheek.

Taking her hand, he tugged her towards the car. 'Come on. Turns out I'm starving.' He winked, promising more than a delicious three-course lunch.

'But what about the trees? I want to see New York at Christmastime. I've never experienced ice skating in Central Park or the Rockefeller Christmas tree.'

'I'll hire someone to plant the damn things for us.' He lengthened his stride, his steps more urgent now he'd made up his mind.

'Are we driving back to London?' She didn't think she'd be able to wait that long with the persistent buzz between her legs.

Car sex...?

'No—I've booked a room at the hotel. We're going to celebrate moving in together. I'm going to lick champagne from every part of your body.'

'I'm not sure I'll survive that experience.'

'You will. It will be fun.'

She nodded. It totally would.

* * * * *

COMING SOON!

We really hope you enjoyed reading this book. If you're looking for more romance, be sure to head to the shops when new books are available on

Thursday
28th June

To see which titles are coming soon, please visit
millsandboon.co.uk

LET'S TALK
Romance

For exclusive extracts, competitions
and special offers, find us online:

f facebook.com/millsandboon

⦿ @millsandboonuk

🐦 @millsandboon

Or get in touch on 0844 844 1351*

For all the latest titles coming soon, visit
millsandboon.co.uk/nextmonth